For Stanley and Bebe,

thanks for inviting me into your home and life. Happy nightmares.

Jasper Dewitt

the patient

the patient

Jasper DeWitt

Houghton Mifflin Harcourt
Boston New York
2020

hmhbooks.com

Library of Congress Cataloging-in-Publication Data

Names: DeWitt, Jasper, author.
Title: The patient / Jasper DeWitt.
Description: Boston : Houghton Mifflin Harcourt, 2020.
Identifiers: LCCN 2019049890 (print) | LCCN 2019049891 (ebook) |
ISBN 9780358181767 (hardcover) | ISBN 9780358309543 |
ISBN 9780358311263 | ISBN 9780358181774 (ebook)
Subjects: GSAFD: Suspense fiction.
Classification: LCC PS3604.E9224 P38 2020 (print) |
LCC PS3604.E9224 (ebook) | DDC 813/.6—dc23
LC record available at https://lccn.loc.gov/2019049890
LC ebook record available at https://lccn.loc.gov/2019049891

Book design by Emily Snyder

Printed in the United States of America

DOC 10 9 8 7 6 5 4 3 2 1

To Roy, who taught me to see the best in myself,
rather than the worst of what others imagined.

the patient

The following manuscript was posted in several installments under the thread "Why I Almost Quit Medicine" on MDconfessions.com, a now-defunct web forum for medical professionals that went off-line in 2012. One of my friends, a Yale graduate from the class of 2011 with an interest in medicine, archived it out of curiosity and was kind enough to share it with me, knowing my interest in ostensibly true horror stories. The original author, as you can see, wrote under a pseudonym, and all attempts to discern his true identity, or those of the other participants in the story, were fruitless, as he appears to have changed multiple identifying details so as to avoid being found out.

March 13, 2008

I write this because, as of now, I am not sure if I am privy to a terrible secret or if I myself am insane. Being a practicing psychiatrist, I realize that would obviously be bad for me both ethically and from a business standpoint. However, since I cannot believe I'm crazy, I'm posting this story because you're probably the only people who would even consider it possible. For me, this is a matter of responsibility to humanity.

Let me say before I start that I wish I could be more specific about the names and places I've mentioned here, but I do need to hold down a job and can't afford to be blacklisted in the medical and mental health fields as someone who goes around spilling the secrets of patients, no matter how special the case. So while the events I describe in this account are true, the names and places have had to be disguised so that I can keep my career safe while also trying to keep my readers safe.

What few specifics I can give are these: My story took place in the early 2000s at a state psychiatric hospital in the United States. My fiancée, Jocelyn, a puckishly intelligent, ferociously conscientious, and radiantly beautiful trust-funder who moonlighted as a Shakespeare scholar, was still mired in her doctoral thesis on the women in *King Lear*. Because of that thesis, and because of my desire to stay as close to her as possible, I had decided to interview only at hospitals in Connecticut.

On the one hand, having gone to one of the most prestigious New England medical schools and followed with an equally rigorous and esteemed residency in the same region, my mentors were particularly adamant on the subject of my next professional step. Appointments at little-known, poorly funded hospitals were for the mere mortals from Podunk State, not doctors with *Lux et Veritas* on their diplomas, and particularly not doctors who had done as well as I had in my studies and clinical training.

I, on the other hand, could not have cared less about such professional one-upmanship. A brush with the ugly side of the mental health system in my childhood, following my mother's institutionalization for paranoid schizophrenia, had made me far more interested in fixing the broken parts of medicine than ensconcing myself in its comfortably functional upper echelons.

But in order to get a job even at the worst hospital, I would need references, which meant that the faculty's prejudices would play a part in my decision-making. One particularly curmudgeonly doctor I turned to happened to know the medical director at the nearby state hospital from his own medical school days. At least, he told me, working under someone with her pedigree would prevent me from learning bad habits, and perhaps our "overactive sense of altruism" would make us a good fit for each other. I readily agreed, partially just to get the reference and partially because the hospital my professor had recommended—a dismal little place I'll call the Connecticut State Asylum (CSA) for the sake of avoiding a lawsuit—suited my preferences perfectly, being one of the most underfunded and ill-starred in the Connecticut health system.

If I hadn't committed to the scientific mind-set that refuses to anthropomorphize natural phenomena, it would've almost seemed that the atmosphere itself was trying to warn me during my first trip up to the hospital for my interview. If you've ever spent time in New England during spring, you know that the weather often turns ugly with no warning because, with apologies to Forrest Gump, the climate in New England is like a box of shit: whatever you get, it's gonna stink.

But even by New England standards, that day was bad. The wind screamed in the trees and slammed against first me and then my car with the violence of a charging bull. The rain pelted my windshield. The road, kept only semi-visible by my windshield wipers, seemed more like a dark charcoal path to purgatory than a thoroughfare, demarcated only with dull yellow and the husks of cars driven by fellow travelers who were more phantoms than actual humans in the wet, gray expanse. The fog choked the air with its forbidding tendrils, some spreading across the pavement, daring the navigator to risk the loneliness of the country road.

As soon as the sign for my exit loomed out of the fog, I turned off and began driving up the first of what felt like a maze of dismal lanes smothered in mist. If not for the trusty set of MapQuest directions I'd printed out, I probably would've gotten lost for hours trying to find my way up the various mountain paths that led, with a serpentine laziness that baffled and mocked the navigator, up the rolling hills to the Connecticut State Asylum.

But if the drive to the place itself felt ill omened, it was nothing compared to the misgivings that struck me when I pulled into the parking lot and saw the campus of the Connecticut State Asylum sprawling before me for the first time. To say the place made a strong and unpleasant impression is the most diplomatic description I can give. The complex was surprisingly vast for a place so underfunded, and radiated the peculiar decay of a once proud institution scarred by neglect. As I drove past row upon row of abandoned, boarded-up ruins that must've once housed wards, some built of faded, crumbling red brick and others of blighted, ivy-eaten brownstone, I could scarcely imagine how anyone could have once worked, let alone lived, in those ghostly tombs that comprised the vast monument to rot that was the Connecticut State Asylum.

Perched at the center of the campus, dwarfing its forsaken brethren, stood the one building that had managed to remain open despite the budget cuts: the main hospital building. Even in its comparatively functional form, that monstrous red-brick pile looked like it was built to do anything but dispel the shadows of the mind. Its towering shape, dominated by severe right angles, with every window a barred rectangular hole, seemed designed to magnify despair and cast more shadows. Even the massive white staircase that led to its doors—the one concession the place made to ornament—looked more like something that had been bleached than painted. As I stared at it, the phantom smell of sterilizing agents floated into my nose. No building I have seen since seemed to so thoroughly embody the stern, bleak lines of arbitrarily enforced sanity.

Paradoxically, the interior of the building was remarkably clean and well kept, if colorless and austere. A bored-looking receptionist aimed me toward the medical director's office on the top floor. The elevator hummed softly for a few moments as you'd expect, before it suddenly and unexpectedly jerked to a halt at the second floor. I braced myself for a fellow passenger as the doors slowly slid open. But it wasn't just one fellow passenger. It was three nurses clustered around a gurney carrying a man. Even though the man was strapped down, I could tell just by looking at him that he wasn't a patient. He wore the uniform of an orderly. And he was *screaming*.

"Let—me—go!" the man roared. "I wasn't done with him!"

Not replying, two of the nurses pushed the gurney into the elevator, where the third—an older woman with her dark hair done up in a ridiculously tight bun—followed him, clucking as she, too, hit the button for the third floor.

"Dear, dear, Graham," she said, her voice carrying a faint lilt that I recognized as Irish, "that's the third time this month. Didn't we tell you about staying out of that room?"

Witnessing this interaction, I naively thought this was a hospital that truly was desperately in need of my knowledge and care. So I wasn't surprised when I was offered the job on the spot, though I experienced a curiously rigorous grilling by Dr. G—, the medical director for the institution, during my interview.

It probably won't shock you that working in a mental hospital, especially an understaffed one, is both fascinating and dreary. The majority of our patients were short-term or outpatient, and their cases ranged from substance abuse and addiction to mood disorders, particularly depression and anxiety-related issues, as well as schizophrenia and psychosis, and even a small group of eating disorders. As a state facility, we have to help everyone who comes to our door, and typically they've bounced through the system quite a bit and are at their wits' end and their financial limits. Changes to the mental health system both political and economic mean that we have only a small long-term ward. Most insurance companies won't pay for sustained care, so these are private patients and wards of the state.

Within the walls of those wards you encounter people with views of the world that would be darkly comical if they weren't causing so much suffering. One of my patients, for instance, tried desperately to tell me that an undergraduate club at a certain elite university was keeping some sort of giant man-eating monster with an unpronounceable name in the basement of a local restaurant, and that this same club had fed his lover to it. In truth, the man had experienced a psychotic break and killed his lover himself. Another patient, meanwhile, was sure that a cartoon character had fallen in love with him and came in for short-term care after he was arrested for stalking the artist. I learned the hard way in my first months that you don't point out reality to people who have delusions. It doesn't help, and they just get angry.

Then there were the three elderly gentlemen, every one of whom thought he was Jesus, which made them all yell at one another anytime they were in the same room. One of them had a background in theology and was a professor at a seminary. He would shout random quotes from Saint Thomas Aquinas at the others, as if this somehow made his claim to the title of Savior more authentic. Again, it would've been funny, if their situations hadn't been so depressingly hopeless.

But every hospital, even one with patients like these, has at least one inmate who's weird even for the mental ward. I'm talking about the kind of person whom even the doctors have given up on and whom everyone gives a wide berth, no matter how experienced they are. This type of patient is obviously insane, but nobody knows how they got that way. What you do know, however, is that it'll drive *you* insane trying to figure it out.

Ours was particularly bizarre. To begin with, he'd been brought into the hospital as a small child and had somehow managed to remain committed for over twenty years, despite the fact that no one had ever succeeded in diagnosing him. He had a name, but I was told that no one in the hospital remembered it, because his case was considered so intractable that no one bothered to read his file anymore. When people had to talk about him, they called him "Joe."

I say talked about him because no one talked *to* him. Joe never came out of his room, never joined group therapy, never had one-on-ones with any psychiatric or therapeutic staff, and pretty much everyone was encouraged to just stay away from him, period. Apparently, any kind of human contact, even with trained professionals, made his condition worse. The only people who saw him regularly were the orderlies who had to change his sheets or drop off and retrieve his meal trays and the nurse who made sure he took his medications. These visits were usually eerily silent and always ended with the staff involved looking like they'd drink the entire stock of a liquor store given the chance. I later learned that Graham, the orderly I'd seen strapped down when I arrived for my interview, had just come from Joe's room that day. As a brand-new staff psychiatrist, I had access to Joe's medical chart and prescriptions, but I saw little information.

It was remarkably thin, seemed to cover only the last year's worth of data, and appeared to be a steady report on the dispensation of mild antidepressants and sedatives. Weirdest of all, his full name was omitted on the charts I was permitted to see, with only the terse sobriquet "Joe" left to identify him.

Being a young, ambitious doctor with a lot in the way of grades and little in the way of modesty, I was fascinated by this mystery patient, and as soon as I heard about him, I made up my mind that I would be the one to cure him. At first I mentioned this only as a sort of passing, half-hearted joke, and those who heard me duly laughed it off as cute, youthful enthusiasm.

However, there was one nurse to whom I confided my wish seriously, the same nurse I'd seen caring for Graham, the orderly. Out of respect for her and for her family, I'll call her Nessie, and it's with her that this story really begins.

I should say a few things about Nessie and why I told her in particular my designs. Nessie had been at the hospital since she'd first emigrated from Ireland as a newly minted nurse in the 1970s. Technically, she was the nursing director and worked only days, but she always seemed to be on hand, so you'd think she lived at the place.

Nessie was an immense source of comfort to me and the other doctors and therapists, because she ran a tight ship that extended not only to the nurses but to the orderlies and custodial staff as well. Nessie seemed to know how to solve practically *any* problem that might arise. If a raging patient needed calming down, Nessie would be there, her fading black hair done up in a no-nonsense bun and her sharp green eyes flashing from her pinched face. If a patient was reluctant to take his medicine, Nessie would be right there to coax him into it. If a member of staff was absent for an unexplained reason, Nessie seemed to always be there to cover for him. If the entire place had burned down, I'm pretty sure Nessie would've been the one to tell the architect how to put it back just the way it had been.

In other words, if you wanted to know how things worked, or wanted advice of any kind, you talked to Nessie. This alone would've been reason enough for me to approach her with my rather naive ambition, but there was one other reason in addition to everything I have said, which is that Nessie was the nurse who'd been tasked with administering medication to Joe and was thus one of the few people who interacted with him on any sort of regular basis.

I remember the conversation distinctly. Nessie was sitting in the hospital cafeteria, holding a paper cup full of coffee in her surprisingly firm hands. I could tell she was in a good mood because her hair was down, and Nessie seemed to adhere to the rule that the more tightly wound she was, the more tightly her hair should be done up. For her to leave it undone meant that she was as relaxed as I'd ever see her.

I filled a cup of coffee for myself, then sat down opposite her. When she noticed me, her face opened into a rare unguarded smile, and she inclined her head in greeting.

"Hullo, Parker. And how's our child prodigy?" she asked, her voice still carrying a slight Irish lilt that made it that much more comforting. I smiled back.

"Apparently suicidal."

"Oh dear," she said with mock concern. "Should I get you a spot of the antidepressants, then?"

"Oh no, nothing like that," I laughed. "No, when I say 'suicidal,' I mean I'm thinking of doing something that everyone else will probably think is very foolish."

"And since it's foolish, you come and speak to the oldest fool on the ward. I see how it is."

"I didn't mean that!"

"Obviously, lad. Don't shite your britches," she said with a calming gesture. "So what is this daredevil stunt you're thinkin' of?"

I leaned in conspiratorially, allowing myself a dramatic pause before answering. "I want to try therapy with Joe."

Nessie, who had also been leaning in to hear what I was saying, sat back so suddenly and frantically you'd think she'd been stung. There was a splash as her coffee cup collided with the floor. She crossed herself, as if by reflex.

"Jesus," she breathed, her full Irish accent flaring up. "Don't go makin' jokes about tha', ye bloody eedjit. Didn't yer mum ever tell ye not teh frighten poor old ladies?"

"I'm not joking, Nessie," I said. "I really—"

"Yes, you bloody well are joking, and that's all you should ever be." Her green eyes were livid now, but I could sense, looking at her, that she wasn't angry at me. She looked like a bear who'd just pulled her cub out of danger. Gently, I put a hand on her arm.

"I'm sorry, Nessie. I didn't mean to scare you."

Her eyes softened, but it didn't make her expression any better. Now she only looked haggard. She placed her hand on mine. "It's not your fault, lad," she said, her accent loosening as the fright faded from her features. "But you don't have any bloody idea what you're talking about, and it's best you never find out."

"Why?" I asked softly. "What's wrong with him?"

Then, knowing she might not answer, I added, "Nessie, you know I'm too smart for my own good. I don't like puzzles I can't solve."

"That's not my fault," she said coldly, her eyes hardening again. "But fine, if it'll stop you, I'll tell you why. Because every time I have to bring medicine into . . . his room, I start to wonder if it wouldn't be worth locking meself up in this 'ospital just to avoid ever 'aving to do it again. I barely sleep from the nightmares I get sometimes. So take my word for it, Parker, if ye're as smart a lad as ye think ye are, ye'll stay away from him. Otherwise, ye might end up in here with him. And none of us wants to see tha'."

I wish I could say her words weren't in vain. But in reality, they only made my curiosity burn hotter, though suffice to say, this was the last time I openly discussed my ambition to cure the mystery patient with a member of staff. But now I had an even better reason: if I could cure him, Nessie and everyone else who had to deal with him would lose what sounded like the main source of misery in their lives. I had to find the records on him and see if I could come up with a diagnosis.

Now, you might be wondering why I didn't ask my boss about the patient and why I would ultimately resort to subterfuge to find the records. The structure of this hospital was such that I rarely saw the medical director who had hired me, Dr. G——. My day-to-day supervisor was a man named Dr. P——, and unfortunately, I knew after meeting him on my first day that we would butt heads. He was a harassed-looking, barrel-chested bear of a man with a shaved head and a beard so wild that it looked like it could have concealed the corpses of several small animals. His eyes, a pair of bored, piggish slits, emanated sourness so intractable that I doubt even winning the lottery would've made him happy. Initially, he verbally harassed me, but I figured out quickly that he was just throwing his weight around to assert his seniority. I later learned that he was profoundly lazy and barely functioned at his job—his approach to all patient care was to drug them 'til they were numb—which left me a tremendous amount of autonomy with my work. Fortunately, the dynamic he wanted was one in which I rarely talked to him, let alone sought his guidance, and no one needed to talk to him about me. As it was, he barely participated in standard team meetings—the near-daily briefings when all hands reviewed patient care plans. I hardly ever even saw him out of his office, where he seemed to hide in a morose funk.

So, back to my hunt for Joe's file. In order to get access to the file of a patient who'd been admitted before the year 2000, I'd need to ask the records clerk to retrieve the paper file using the patient's last name as a reference point. This was because the hospital hadn't digitized anything beyond patients' names and dates of admission before the year 2000. Searching by first name or date of admission was theoretically possible, but I was told that unless I wanted the records clerks to kill me, I should avoid asking them to do this.

Eventually, I hit on a solution opportunistically. I snuck a look at Nessie's meds-and-duty roster during a rare moment when she left it unguarded. To my immense gratification, this document seemed to be the one place that listed Joe's full name: Joseph E. M—.

Hoping to avoid the gossipy weekday records clerk who was always snippy even when I needed to check records for legitimate reasons, I went in on a weekend when Jerry, a barely functional alcoholic, was working in the records room. He let me in, gave me directions on where to go, and slurred at me that I'd better "put the f—king files back" when I was done before slouching back in his chair.

And then I had it. Joseph E. M— had been first admitted in 1973 at the age of six, and he was marked as still in hospital custody. The file was so covered in dust that I doubted anyone had opened it in a decade and so thick that it looked like it might burst.

But the clinical notes were still there, and in surprisingly good condition, along with a crude black-and-white photo of a fair-haired boy giving the camera a wide-eyed, feral stare. The image made me feel unsafe, just looking at it. Averting my eyes, I turned to the notes and started scanning them.

As I read, I realized that the reports that Joe's condition was undiagnosed had been misstating the truth. It wasn't that there was no diagnosis. It was that there had been a couple but Joe's symptoms seemed to mutate unpredictably. Most surprising of all, however, Joe had actually been discharged at one point, very early in his life in the mental health system, after staying only forty-eight hours in the hospital. Here are the full contents of the physician's notes at the time:

June 5, 1973

Patient Joseph M— is a six-year-old boy suffering from acute night terrors, including vivid hallucinations of some sort of creature that lives in the walls of his room and which emerges at night to frighten him. Joseph's parents brought him in after one particularly violent episode in which his arms sustained significant contusions and abrasions. Patient claims it was from the creature's claws. May indicate a proclivity for self-harm. Prescribed: 50 mg of Trazodone, along with some basic therapy.

June 6, 1973

The patient has been cooperative in therapy session. He suffers from acute entomophobia and possible audiovisual hallucinations. He experienced no sleep disturbances last night but explained that this was only because the monster "doesn't live here." However, when presented with the theory that the monster was a part of his own psyche, patient was very receptive, which suggests nothing more serious than normal childhood fears. Have suggested to parents that we monitor the patient for an additional 24 hours and possibly start him on a mild course of antipsychotics if we see further evidence of hallucinations. They were receptive.

I almost laughed. It seemed ridiculous that such a brief set of entries would become the prelude to decades of horror. Nevertheless, I pressed on. The notes indicated that Joe was discharged after the additional twenty-four hours as promised. There was also a reference to an audiotape of Joe's one therapy session, the number of which I was careful to write down in the notebook I'd brought with me.

However, the doctor's optimism after Joe's first visit had obviously been misplaced, because Joe was back the next day, this time with a much more serious set of disorders. And this time, he was never discharged. The notes from his second admittance follow:

June 8, 1973

Patient Joseph M— is a six-year-old boy previously admitted for night terrors. A course of sedatives and some rudimentary coping techniques were prescribed. Patient's condition has since changed dramatically. No longer shows signs of previous entomophobia or possible hallucinations. Instead, patient seems to have regressed to a preverbal state.

Patient additionally shows a high propensity toward violence and sadism. Patient has assaulted numerous members of staff and has had to be restrained. Despite relative youth, patient seems intuitively aware of which parts of the human body are most vulnerable or sensitive to pain. This may even be true on a strictly individual level. Patient kicked one older nurse in the shin, where she had recently had surgery. Nurse had to be removed in a wheelchair.

Patient is no longer cooperative with therapy. Emits clicking and scratching noises instead of talking and is no longer capable of bipedal movement. He remains violent and had to be restrained and removed after attempting to assault Dr. A—.

June 9, 1973

Patient's condition has changed again. When nurse Ashley N— told patient that he was "a bad little boy for kicking and punching so much," patient suddenly became verbal. He proceeded to abuse Ms. N— verbally, calling her "a long-nosed Christ-killer," a "dumb k– bitch," etc. Ms. N— became acutely distressed and subsequently requested leave, citing traumatic memories triggered by patient's insults.

Patient's targeted physical violence, verbal abuse, and antisocial behavior all suggest a form of antisocial personality disorder normally too sophisticated for someone his age. Specific personal insights on the part of patient not yet explainable.

June 10, 1973

Patient's condition continues to deteriorate. When brought in for a review, patient made no attempt to engage but instead commenced verbally abusing psychiatrist. Referred to psychiatrist as a "f—king worthless drunk," a "sexless cold fish," and "bitch boy Tommy," among others. These insults all correspond to personal attacks previously suffered by psychiatrist at moments of acute mental distress. Asked patient why he chose these insults. Patient refused to answer. Asked patient if anyone had called him anything like this. Patient refused to answer. Asked patient why he chose to verbally assault people this way. Patient said he had to, because he was "a bad little boy." Asked patient if he could stop being a bad little boy. Patient asked what *I* thought. I asked patient what he thought. Patient refused to answer. Patient released from therapy. On a personal note, I wish only to comment that one therapy session with this boy made me more tempted to break my 20-year Alcoholics Anonymous pledge than

```
any other experience I have had in that
time. Consequently, I am asking that an-
other psychiatrist take over this case.
```

No entries on Joe's treatment followed this one. Apparently, one session had been enough to make the writer give up in disgust. I shook my head. Even an understaffed hospital should put in more effort than this. Indeed, the only item from the same year was a curt note from the medical director ordering staff to keep Joe isolated from the rest of the population. For four years after that, there was nothing.

March 15, 2008

Whoa. I seriously didn't expect my first post to get this much attention. I honestly expected you guys to think I was exaggerating. And, yeah, I know that's been the response of some (I hear you, DrHouse1982), but the overall positivity of the response so far has truly floored me.

I also underestimated how hard it would be to write all of this down, though the fact that all of you seem so ready to believe it, and even speculate about what was going on, is somewhat comforting. I have read your comments, and while I can tell you right now that none of you are even close to realizing just how fucked this patient was (you don't have even half the story yet), it's nice to see that people will take an account like this seriously. There might be hope after all.

Anyway, where was I? Oh yeah, Joe's file, and the fact that it basically went dark for four years.

The file started up again in 1977. This time, sections of each entry had been redacted, with a note preceding it saying to see Dr. G— for the unredacted file. It seemed that funding cuts forced the staff to make patients share rooms. As such, there was a note from the new medical director, Dr. A—, instructing staff to find roommates who seemed unlikely to trigger whatever Joe's condition was.

The staff evidently failed at this.

The next memo that bore any content was also from Dr. A— and was addressed to a Dr. G—, known to me as the medical director. It ran like this:

December 14, 1977

I don't know whose idea it was to move Philip A— into Joe's room, but whoever it is, I want them fired. Putting a grown man with such serious anger issues in a room with a boy who's got such a powerful need to push people's buttons was obviously not going to have positive results. So now it seems we have at least one patient whose family might press charges if they ever find out what their son has been through. I take it you've heard the stories already about Philip needing to be sedated before he could make good on his promise to "kill

> the little f—king monster." I don't know what this will do to Joe's condition, but I can't imagine it'll be good.

Apparently, Joe was transferred to a conventional hospital for a broken arm, bruised ribs, a concussion, and a fractured skull. After this first disaster, records indicated that when Joe returned, he was paired with someone closer to his age: an eight-year-old boy who'd been admitted for issues associated with his severe autism. This led to a much worse result.

> December 16, 1977
>
> Our insurer will not be happy if we get more incidents like the one with Will A—. The one bit of good news, I suppose, is that the autopsy shows no signs of foul play. Joe's violent tendencies must've been toned down a bit. But even if the autopsy will probably absolve us of any blame, I worry that a good attorney will pick it apart in court. When was the last time an eight-year-old died of heart failure? Check with the nurse and pray we didn't give Will too strong a dose of something.

Joe's next roommate was a boy of six who'd been admitted with post-traumatic stress disorder resulting from his father's sexual abuse. There was a note next to the new rooming arrangement instructing orderlies and nurses to periodically look in on the two because the boy had a tendency to become violent. As it happened, he was the one who benefited from this protection.

December 18, 1977

Patient Nathan I— moved into joint room with patient Joseph M—. At 10 p.m., Nathan and Joe are locked in for lights-out. At 1:34 a.m., patient Nathan can be heard sobbing and screaming. At 1:36 a.m., orderly Byron R— enters room to find Joe on top of Nathan, in the process of sexual assault. Patient Nathan is removed and patient Joe is restrained and placed in solitary confinement. Patient Nathan has sustained bruising, multiple bites, and slight rectal tearing. He was moved to another facility for medical treatment. Patient Joe will be kept in solitary confinement for a week. All staff will be reminded not to discuss sexual matters within earshot of underage patients. Termination of all orderlies except for orderly R— is *strongly* suggested.

The last roommate Joe had who was drawn from the general population of mental patients was a teenage meth addict who'd developed severe paranoid personality disorder, probably picked because he could have easily overpowered Joe if the boy tried to assault him. What's more, as a further precaution against that sort of assault, the two were placed in a room where they could be permanently restrained, to stop them from hurting each other.

However, this didn't turn out any better.

December 20, 1977

Firstly, have someone look into getting us stronger straps for our beds. After what happened last night with Claude Y—, and everything else that's happened this past week, we're going to need to assure the public that nothing of the kind will happen again. Also, get the orderlies to go over the room one more time, because I am frankly incredulous at the explanation they're giving us. I don't care how paranoid Claude was; there's nothing in that room that could scare him enough to make him chew through multiple leather straps and throw himself out the window. The straps would be hard enough, even with an average adrenaline rush. But to force open a barred window? There had to be something wrong with the bars, or the bed, or the window.

One way or another, though, I mean to find out what that child is doing to make accidents like this happen. Assign any orderly you want to stay with him tomorrow night. Make sure the orderly has anything he needs to defend himself.

> Treat this as a case of a criminally insane patient, even though we can't prove that much of anything's happened beyond the Nathan incident. Oh, and get the orderly to take a tape recorder in. If that little bastard so much as breathes, I want it available for analysis.

There was another record indicating where to find the audiotape that resulted from this order. I jotted its number down as well. There was one final communication from Dr. A—— on the subject of Joe, and in it, I finally found at least a partial answer for why the staff so despaired of diagnosing and treating this particular patient. But unlike the previous documents, this wasn't a memo. It was a handwritten note, apparently preserved by Dr. G——.

> *Dear Rose,*
>
> *I just spoke to Frank. I think it's fair to say he's not going to be ready for work for at least a month, considering the state he's in. And you know what? I'm actually going to let him have that time as paid sick leave, because it's my fault he's like that. Can't punish someone for following your own orders. Mind you, if he's not better by the time it's over, we'll have to keep him here.*
>
> *I've also come to a conclusion: Whatever Joe has, I'm sure we can't cure it. I don't even think we can diagnose it. It's obviously not in the DSM. And given the effect he has on others, I'm starting to doubt that anyone could diagnose him.*

You know what? I'm getting ahead of myself. First, let's talk about what Frank told me. He says that Joe just kept whispering to him the entire night. That's it. Just whispering. But it wasn't a child's normal voice. Somehow the boy managed to make his voice go all guttural and hoarse, and he kept trying to remind Frank of things they'd done together—like he knew him from somewhere.

But the thing is, Rose, the things Joe was trying to remind Frank of? They were all nightmares Frank had as a child. He said it was like the monster in those nightmares had been whispering to him all night, saying how much he missed chasing him, and catching him, and eating him.

It sounded outlandish. How would a boy that young know what a 40-year-old orderly used to dream about? So I listened to the tape. And I can't come to any other conclusion but that he imagined it. I didn't hear a sound, and the microphone was turned all the way up. What's more, Joe was restrained all the way on the other side of the room, so if he was making a sound loud enough for Frank to hear, the mic would've picked it up. I don't think he could've avoided that unless he was whispering right into Frank's ear, which is obviously impossible.

Even weirder, after a bit, I was able to hear Frank breathing very loudly. And his breathing patterns weren't normal. It sounded like he was hyperventilating. Like he was having a panic attack, in fact. But I listened to it over and over again, and there were no other sounds. At all. So I have no idea what Frank's talking about.

I now know for sure, after this session and the one I had with Joe that we can't cure him. It'll take a better doctor than me to figure him out, and good luck finding one who'll be willing to come work in this shithole. Maybe he'll die in here. But there's nothing we can do.

Rose, you're going to be medical director one day. We both know it. We've discussed it at length. I know you think this is your fault. I know you'll be tempted to keep trying new things with him. Don't. Just keep him here at his parents' expense and feed them whatever story you have to. They're rich enough to afford a lifetime of care. Even if they somehow go broke, find room in the budget. I couldn't have it on my conscience if I knew I'd had him in my care and he somehow got out to cause trouble in the real world with whatever he has just because we failed. Promise me, Rose.

—Thomas

After this letter, there was only an official document stating that all therapy with Joe would stop. He would have his own room, but at the price of being kept restrained in it twenty-four hours a day, seven days a week. Only a select few orderlies would be allowed in to change his sheets and deliver his meals, and only the most experienced nurse would be given the task of administering medication to him. All staff would be encouraged to stay away from him. He would not be referred to except by the extremely nondescript shortened name, so that anyone wanting to find out more information wouldn't know where to start. It was, in brief, everything that I'd observed since arriving at my new workplace.

Even so, if I'd been intrigued before, I was hooked now. Here lay the possibility of discovering a previously undocumented disorder—not merely a permutation of something already in the *DSM*, but something entirely new! And I had patient zero under this hospital's roof. My choice of residency began to seem almost an act of God. There was just one thing to do now: listen to the audiotapes I'd seen referenced in the records.

I immediately went back to the records clerk and showed him the numbers for the tapes, expecting to get them fairly quickly. However, to my surprise, after he'd typed in the numbers on his computer, he furrowed his brow in confusion and then walked back into the records room without a word. Some ten minutes later, he returned looking even more confused.

"There's nothing under those numbers, doc," he said. "Never has been. You sure you wrote them down right?"

I was quite certain I had, and anyway, I couldn't risk another trip that could alert him to which file I'd been looking at. Besides, if they had ever been there, it would make sense that they might have been destroyed or removed given their connection to the hospital's biggest problem patient. I faked a tired grin and shook my head at the records clerk.

"Someone's played a joke on me," I said. "Sorry for wasting your time."

I walked out of the records office and discreetly left the hospital. Knowing I would need time to think about what I'd just read, I decided to stop at a coffee shop before heading back home. While there, I began to jot down my own makeshift notes, so as to keep what I had read fresh in my mind for later analysis. These notes have formed the basis for my re-creation of the file in the preceding pages.

It was obvious that Joe had started with some sort of empathy-based disorder, which perhaps had been worsened by the concussion he sustained at the hands of his first roommate. Had he merely been a nasty little kid who pushed people's buttons at random, it would've been easy to diagnose him as a textbook case of antisocial personality disorder.

But the thing is, Joe's empathy problems seemed to run in different and equally extreme directions. His emotional empathy—that is, the ability to feel what other people were feeling—was obviously nonexistent if he'd been making people kill themselves and trying to rape a boy before he even knew what rape was. But his cognitive empathy—the ability to recognize what others were feeling—must've been unbelievable. Almost superhuman. Not only could he spot another person's insecurities, but he could predict with perfect accuracy how to exploit them in order to cause maximum distress. It was the kind of skill I'd have expected to see in a trained CIA interrogator, not something spontaneously developed by a young child.

More puzzling still had been his apparent shift in tactics right after his disastrous encounter with his first roommate. Prior to that, the numerous therapy records all indicated that his preferred approach was to induce feelings of anger or self-hatred in his victims. Yet immediately afterward, as if his modus operandi had changed, he'd switched to inducing fear so extreme it would trigger a fight-or-flight response. Why this sudden shift in approach? What had happened to change his symptoms? And who's to say it was even him who'd triggered those feelings of fear in the first place? What about the fact that the orderly's recording of his encounter with Joe revealed only silence?

That night, probably because of the reference to the orderly's negative experience, one of my childhood nightmares resurfaced. I wouldn't ordinarily go into it since it raises terrible memories for me, but it's relevant to what happened later, so I'd better explain.

My mother was sent to the hospital for paranoid schizophrenia when I was ten. My father had put her there after the night he'd woken to find her bending over the kitchen table with the sharpest knife we owned buried clean through her wrist, muttering about demon insects that the devil had put in her ears to make her hear the screams of the damned. She thought that cutting herself would make the insects bleed out of her and she'd stop hearing the voices. I wasn't aware of any of this at the time. My dad told me that he'd made damn sure I was out of the house whenever Mom had an episode, which, in retrospect, explains why he was so cool about letting me constantly go to sleepovers at my friends' houses. But even at that age, I knew something was wrong, and I wasn't surprised when I woke one morning to find my dad at the kitchen table, stern and sad as he explained to me that my mother had to go away.

But, obviously, I missed my mom and started begging my dad to take me to see her. For the longest time, he refused, but eventually he relented and took me to St. Christina's, the hospital where Mom had ended up. That one visit nearly broke me, and it completely quenched any desire I had to see my mother again.

To give you some context, St. Christina's is one of those poor, urban hospitals that has always been underfunded and which suffers from reports of patient abuse right up to the present day. In the eyes of the local government, it was effectively a dumping ground for human trash, and the city I came from doesn't spend much time worrying about the comfort of those it sees as garbage.

Fortunately, my dad was gainfully employed and could afford to keep my mother from pushing a cart down a street and screaming at random passersby, but only just. So St. Christina's was our one option. Being a kid, I didn't understand that some hospitals were better than others. Until that visit.

My mother was housed in a small side building where the most financially strapped patients were kept, and long before I got to her room, I knew I categorically did not belong there. The place was held behind two heavy, ugly, gray doors, and they opened with a buzz that sounded like it had been calculated to disrupt the human mind before you entered. The lobby, meanwhile, was little more than a grimy cube, with chairs that even bedbugs wouldn't deign to touch.

Some of the patients, each clad in identical filthy hospital gowns, wandered freely in the surrounding halls, throwing jackrabbit stares and subterranean-sounding mutters at the sane visitors. Even at ten, I could feel the rage and fright in those eyes, which seemed to scream in their sockets. *Why are you here, among the damned, you poor dumbass child? Didn't your momma tell you this is no place for you?*

But my momma was one of the damned. I found that out as soon as we got to her room and the orderly opened the door. In that moment, I was hit with the overpowering smell of urine and blood, and even the orderly covered his nose in reflexive disgust before shouting for his peers. Not knowing that something was wrong, I pattered into the room.

My mother was crouched against the wall, her gown soaked in a slowly spreading pool of her own urine. Clutched in her hand was a small, makeshift shiv that she'd stuck halfway into her wrist, from which bright red blood was weeping. Momma must've felt my eyes on her, because she turned toward me as I stared, and her mouth split into a smile so wide I was surprised her cheeks didn't split open. An ugly, blackish-purple bruise marred her forehead, probably from banging her head against the wall.

"Parker, child," she murmured. "Come help me with this. The damn maggots won't crawl out of me, baby."

I had no idea what to say. I had no idea even what to think. I stood there and stared at the abomination that had once been my mother. Seeing my expression, which must've been blazing with shock and revulsion, my mother's face fell, and she dropped the shiv. Her wrist still pouring blood, she raised her face to the ceiling and let out an animal howl that slowly devolved into peals of laughter. Or sobs. I honestly couldn't tell which. Then, slowly, she began to crawl toward me, the blood from her wrist joining with the urine on the floor to form a hideous puce broth around her. Some part of her must have remembered she was a mother, and that her child was afraid, because she began to croon a lullaby softly, in a voice hoarse with months of misery.

"Hush-a-bye, baby, on the tree tops," she rasped. "When the wind blows, the cradle will rock. When the bough breaks, the cradle will f-f-faaaaalll . . ."

There was the sound of heavy footfalls behind me, and two orderlies rushed past, one of them holding a syringe in his hand. She was still singing—and laughing—as they seized her and shoved her onto the bed.

"When the bough breaks, the cradle will fall!" she shrieked. "And down will come ba—"

The syringe had gone in, and she went quiet. I turned and ran, into the open arms of my father, who held me as I wept with primal, uncomprehending terror.

You need to know this because you must understand that this was the day I decided to become a psychiatrist. And not just any psychiatrist, but one who would never treat any patient as disposable, no matter how hopeless or unlovable they seemed.

Which brings me back to the nightmare I had after reading Joe's file. One of the least surprising effects of a traumatic experience is having bad dreams about that experience afterward, particularly when your brain is as underdeveloped as mine was during that fateful encounter with my mom. As you can probably tell from reading this, I still grapple with the feeling that I have an obligation to help any and every person who has been left to suffer from their own mental illness, simply because some part of me still questions whether it was my fault that my mother went insane in the first place. True, blaming myself like that is irrational, but kids—and adults who are still processing childhood trauma—don't blame themselves simply out of a secret desire for self-hatred. They blame themselves so they can feel in control of what seems like an impossible situation, because the only way to feel like they can process it is to reclaim their agency, even by blaming themselves for something they have no control over.

I like to think that as I have gotten older, I have grown more capable of dealing with the trauma of that experience without feeling the need to hold myself to an impossible standard in order to feel in control. But that wasn't true at first, which is probably where the nightmare I'm about to describe came in.

In the dream, everything began just as it had in real life. I walked into St. Christina's and took a seat in the dismal waiting room. Only there was no one there besides me. In fact, in the dream, I somehow knew the entire building was empty except for me. And it. The thing I called my mother.

I could feel its presence in the building without even seeing or hearing it. That awful, traumatic wrongness vibrated in every inch of wall, chair, and ratty carpet I could see. And even though I would have given anything to stand up and run away from it, and out of that miserable, crumbling monument to the personal hells of broken souls, what I wanted to do and what the dream let me do were completely different things. So instead of running, I felt myself stand as if bewitched and walk slowly, step by step, across the stained gray linoleum floor to the room that housed my mother.

Even before I got there, I could hear her laughing. A high, keening, mirthless cackle of the damned that made the walls seem to literally contract around me like the walls of a boa constrictor's stomach. The closer I got to its room, the more desperately I fought to turn away, and the more I fought, the faster the dream forced me to approach. As I reached the doorway beyond which the hell of my own childhood trauma was gibbering, the smell of piss and blood blew into my nostrils and choked off my air, even as the dream forced me, with implacable, merciless force, to look at the cause of the sounds and smells.

My mother was, as she had been in real life, crouched against the wall of her—its—lair, its dirty hospital gown soaked to the skin beneath the waist from the slowly spreading pool of urine underneath it. As I entered the cell, it sensed my presence and raised its leering face to mine.

And this is where my subconscious managed to somehow transform the already terrible details of that memory into the true, hallucinogenic stuff of nightmares. My mother's smile was not merely wide and manic—it was so wide that her cheeks had split, revealing bleeding gums that leaked their hideous scarlet effluvia down onto her chin and gown. Her arms were not merely sliced open in brutal, jagged cuts from the shiv; the wounds festered and crawled with maggots. And where my actual mother had appeared tall only by comparison to my childlike frame, the nightmare mother was so tall that she couldn't stand upright in the cell but loomed over me as she bent against the ceiling, a spider already gushing with the blood of the traumatized fly in its web.

Then it screamed. Normally, I was saved from hearing much of this because I would scream in response and wake myself up. But for whatever reason, the night after I found Joe's file, my mind would not let my throat form the necessary sound. Instead, I was forced to choke out terrified, rasping noises as that endless perdition-laced howl reverberated through every chamber of my ears. How long this went on I couldn't say, as dream time eludes the most strict clock, but the mental distress I felt was so acute that it may as well have been hours.

Yet this was not the only terrible surprise that my subconscious mind had in store for me. There was one more fresh horror. As I watched the nightmare mother shriek at me, the mire beneath its feet suddenly began to bubble as if boiling over. Then, suddenly, from within the depths of that feculent, squalid pond, a pair of feelers shot out and wrapped themselves with dreadful tightness around my mother. The feelers looked to be made of tangled black hair and blood-stained leather, but they moved and jerked like tentacles attached to some awful subterranean horror. As they dragged the nightmare mother to her knees and into the muck below, she began to shrink, her wounds healed, and her face assumed the look of frustrated love that my mother—my *real* mother—had worn as she tried to comfort me.

"Oh, my darling boy," my mother crooned. "My sweet baby . . ."

The dream permitted no attempt at aid from me. Instead, I was forced to watch as that awful pair of bristling feelers dragged my mother into what now looked like a lake of her own filth. When her head finally reached the surface, I heard a terrible sound: a burbling, hacking laugh echoing from beneath the pond that rang with increasingly deranged sadism as the feelers yanked the last remnants of my mother into its depths. Somehow, the sight made my brain release my throat, and I screamed out at her.

"Mommy! Mommy! Come back! Mo—"

"Parker! *Parker!*"

I felt someone shaking me, and, just like that, the dream blinked out of my mind, and I found myself staring into the bleary, very frightened, and yet fiercely loving eyes of Jocelyn.

March 18, 2008

Hey, guys. Nice to see the reception growing. And thank you for your feedback. No, I can't do anything for her anymore. My mother passed while I was still rather young, which further compounds my inability to help her. And she's really not what this story is about. I just needed you to know that piece of my history.

Fortunately, the dream didn't recur that night, and I more or less forgot about it as I returned to the hospital. Having read the case file, I fully intended to see if there was some way I could get an audience with our mysterious problem patient. I was debating how to go over my supervisor's head, since I knew he would slam the door on this. When he had given me his tour of the premises as part of my orientation, he deliberately did not even walk to Joe's end of the hallway. When I asked him about it, he bit my head off and told me to mind my own patients and never interfere unsolicited with another psychiatrist's work. "You can't help *everyone*." So I needed to find a justification for going over his head. But as I arrived at the hospital, a new distraction presented itself.

A crowd had assembled around the main hospital entrance, including more than a few people whose cameras and microphones positively identified them as reporters. Immediately curious as to what was going on, I fought my way through the crowd, only to see a stretcher bearing a body bag being loaded into a police van. Worried, I scanned the crowd for any face I might recognize and spotted an orderly whom I'd seen working on the same ward as me. I fought my way over to him and asked what had happened.

"Nessie died." His voice sounded hollow, as if he were a million miles away. "They're saying she threw herself off the roof last night after making her rounds. No one knows why, but one of the patients says she did it after she'd finished . . . you know, with *him*."

Now just as horrified as my counterpart, I reached out and gave him a stiff, one-armed hug, as if to reassure him that someone else felt the same thing he did. He didn't react. Apparently, the shock was still too strong.

And just like that, my need to cure Joe became personal.

Note: The next update will take place on Friday. We're getting closer to the stuff I find really difficult to talk about, so my writing pace is probably going to slow.

March 21, 2008

Oh, man, I knew I was throwing a grenade into this thread with that last post, but I didn't expect *this.* For God's sake, the mods stickied this post at the top of the forum! I never expected my little confessional to get that much attention, or that much love, and I can't tell you all how much I appreciate it. I've also been more than a little amused reading all your attempts to diagnose Joe, even though none of you are even close to the truth. But reading your comments has made it easier to remember all the shit that other doctors ruled out, which in turn has made it easier to remember more details.

I haven't even gotten to the bit that makes me doubt my sanity yet, and already the memories are making me feel like I have to drink more and more just to sit down and write. My wife's worried about me, but once I told her what this was all about, she understood. She's the only other one I've told, and whether out of love, or open-mindedness, she believes me. I'm still glad to see that so many of you do, too, and after the last part, some of you at least seem to be getting closer to the truth. I don't think anyone could figure the whole thing out, though. Not now. You simply don't have enough information.

Anyway, I left off with Nessie's suicide and how it shocked so many people.

Frankly, it should have. Even though I'd been there only a short time, I knew the loss of a nurse like Nessie would be felt for years to come. Over the days that followed the dreadful event, it became obvious that the ward I worked on had trouble functioning at all when there was no Nessie around to carry most of the workload. The police didn't help either, as they made a point of questioning every single member of staff, which slowed us down even more and raised a lot of uncomfortable suspicions about foul play. But, ultimately, the case was cleared as a suicide, and they finally left us alone.

For the sake of order on the ward, Dr. P—— was forced to step up and act more in control of the staff he theoretically already supervised. His aggressive new participation manifested as yelling at me to stop wasting my time on talk therapy with my patients, that's what the group sessions were for, and just medicate them so they'd be quiet. A more easily cowed doctor probably would've just taken it, but I didn't. Instead, I asked Dr. P— to visit my patients if he thought my methods weren't working, because otherwise, I'd make sure to put it in writing that he'd asked me to do something ineffective. He raged and stormed at this and called me something I won't print here, but eventually, he relented, since he knew that the patients under my care had been receiving more targeted prescriptions and were benefiting from my more expansive attention.

"You've made your point," he snarled. "But everyone has to pull more weight around here with Nessie dead. If your methods can't accommodate that, then find someplace else to work."

He wasn't wrong about the "pulling more weight" thing, and damn my bravery, because I sent him an unsolicited memo detailing the extra patients and triage details I'd be willing to take on, to lighten his load. I named two additional patients suffering from severe depression and, more importantly, included the name "Joseph M—" on my list.

The next day, I arrived early, and seeing that I'd beaten Dr. P— to the hospital, I slid the manila envelope carrying my list under his door. Two hours later, Dr. P— arrived at the hospital, all bluster and discontent as usual, and without so much as acknowledging any other staff members, opened the door to his office and strode inside. There was the sound of crinkling paper, and I saw him hesitate slightly, then reach down for something at floor level. I walked away hastily and immersed myself in a proper task. Whatever Dr. P——'s reaction would be, I wanted to give him at least a few minutes before I had to bear the—

"Parker Goddamn H——!"

The sound of Dr. P——'s voice rang like a great husky bell. Oh boy, this was going to get interesting. I heard angry footfalls approach my office, and then Dr. P——'s face poked around my doorframe, scarlet with shock and anger.

"My office, wonder boy! *Now!*"

I stood up, willing myself to stay calm, and followed him, feeling sweat begin to form on my hands. I clenched them and sat down opposite Dr. P——'s desk, trying my best to give him a look of pure serenity.

Dr. P—— picked up my list of new patients and practically threw it across the desk at me.

"What is this?" he asked, stabbing the name "Joseph M——" with one fat finger. "What the *hell* is this?!"

I shrugged. "You asked me to carry a heavier load. I'm volunteering my energy."

Dr. P——'s breathing sharpened from the effort to remain calm. "How did you get this name?" he asked slowly. "Who told you we had a patient with this name? Do you have any idea *who this is?*"

"Yes, I know who it is. I found out from Nessie." Which was *technically* true.

Dr. P—'s eyes contracted into two angry lines. "Do you know anything about this patient?"

"Yes, and I want to treat him."

"*No!* You don't, and you fucking won't. You don't know *anything* about him. You just want to prove you're King Shit of Fuck Mountain. Well, you have gone too goddamn *far,* Parker. Here's what's going to happen now. You will leave this office. You will *never* mention this again. *Ever.* Or I will personally make sure you are fucking fired and sent back to those Reaganomicals in New Haven with your tail between your legs, *got it?!*"

"That's enough, Bruce."

I jumped. The cool, razor-sharp voice that had come from the office doorway behind me belonged to none other than Dr. G—. Dr. P—, who had been leaning over his desk so as to menace me more effectively, suddenly went pale and fell backward into his chair.

"Rose," he said. "What are you—I mean, always a pleasure to have you on the ward, but why—"

"Because I need to see someone," Dr. G— replied smoothly, sweeping into the office with regal iciness.

"That is, if you've finished giving him a reason to file an HR complaint about you?"

"Oh," said Dr. P——. "Well . . . I mean . . ."

"Out, Bruce."

"I was just—"

"Words fail to express how much I don't care. Out."

"Wait . . . this . . . this is my office."

"And I need your desk for a few minutes."

Dr. P——, looking deflated, stood up and began to exit. However, as he did, something seemed to nag at him, and he turned to me with a look that seemed at once full of rage and pity.

"You dumb goddamn kid," he snarled. "I'm trying to protect you. You've done good work here. I hate to admit it, but you have. Get away from this before it's too—"

"Out, Bruce. *Now.*"

Dr. P—— gave me a last pained glance and exited his office. I was left alone with Dr. G——, who crossed to Dr. P——'s desk and sat down, giving me a look of wary interest. As she sat, her eye caught my proposed list of new patients, and her mouth quirked into a grim smile as she read it.

I realize I've never described Dr. G——. Judging by the dates on the file I'd seen, she had to be at least in her early fifties, but she didn't look a day over forty, with shoulder-length auburn hair, piercing green eyes, and a round but slightly pinched face. She was also very tall—taller than me with the help of the pair of businesslike black heels she was wearing—and rail thin, with a body that looked more like it belonged to an Olympic athlete than a doctor. If I'd been older, I probably would have found her attractive, but as it was, her hawklike stare only had the effect of making me aware of how painfully young and inexperienced I was. It was like being X-rayed by a very judgmental machine.

After a few moments of considering me, she spoke. "I suppose this was inevitable. So, tell me. Why do you want to attempt therapy on an incurable patient?"

"Well," I said, "I'm not so sure he's incurable."

"How would you know? Have you spoken to him?"

"No."

"Why not?"

I gaped at her. "I mean, I assumed that if I so much as tried, I'd be fired, what with everyone threatening me if I didn't stay away."

"Who threatened you?"

"Well . . . Dr. P——, as you can see. And Nessie."

"Ah," said Dr. G——. "Well, even if she took every other duty on herself, I can promise you that Nessie O'S—— did not have firing authority. You could have just taken the key and visited Joe whenever you liked."

I blinked. "You mean there isn't some special procedure?"

"Oh, to *treat* him, yes," said Dr. G—. "But to simply walk into his room? No. I think some combination of fear of Bruce, fear of Nessie, and fear of the stories about Joe himself just keep most people away. Those that do go in rarely stay for more than a few minutes unless they have to, and those that have to . . . well, you saw what happened to Nessie."

"Yeah," I said. "I did."

She cocked her head at me. "And that doesn't dissuade you? You're not afraid of ending up the same way?"

"No," I said. "If anything, what she did made it personal."

"I see," said Dr. G—. "Well, next question, then. You haven't spoken to Joe. Have you seen his file?"

"No," I said just as quickly, yet something I said must've given away the lie, because she glared at me.

"I have better things to do than listen to a junior physician lie to me. Try the truth next time, or this meeting's over.

I swallowed. "Fine," I said. "Yes."

"Better. So if you read that and still want to work with him, you must have a diagnosis in mind. Care to enlighten me as to what you saw that the rest of us missed after twenty years of looking?"

It was a trap. "I don't think you missed anything," I said carefully. "But the file says he was last treated in the late '70s. The *DSM*'s been revised since then, as you know."

"Stop patronizing me and get to the point."

Gulp. "I think your first diagnosis might have been right, and we might just be dealing with a very, very sophisticated sociopath. More sophisticated than we knew they could get in the '70s. There's obviously also sadistic personality disorder, and he may have some sort of psychological progeria, which makes him seem more adult. The oddest thing is his ability to induce delusions in those around him, which is rare, but possible. Alternately, I think you might also want to test if he has some sort of disorder with how he mirrors people's emotions—"

She put up a hand to stop me. "Wrong. I don't blame you for trying, but still wrong. And to be fair, you couldn't have gotten the answer right anyway. You haven't seen the file."

I raised an eyebrow. "Didn't you just make me confess that I had?"

"What you've seen isn't the full file. I'm not stupid. I know people find a way to game the records system every few years and look at what's down there. So rather than remove his file, I just left an incomplete set of documents there, knowing it would scare off almost anyone who got access out of curiosity. What you've seen is what I wanted you to see. Nothing more."

I blinked stupidly. "How much more is there?"

"The remaining documents are a bit more hands-on and technical than what you've seen. And then, of course, there are the two audiotapes. Which, speaking of those, that's how I knew you were lying. Because anytime someone requests those file numbers, our records clerks all know to drop me a note. They don't know why to do it, but I'm sure you can figure it out."

"The only way someone would know the numbers is if they'd seen the file," I said dejectedly.

She nodded. "Which means that I knew you'd seen it before I walked in here."

She leaned back in Dr. P——'s chair and gave me a satisfied, piercing look. I wondered if this was how a mouse felt when being stared down by a cat.

"So," she said briskly, "since we've established that I am the one in this room who has access to the greater share of knowledge, tell me, aside from assuming we were too stupid to see something just because it wasn't in the *DSM* yet or haven't considered that he suffers from a cocktail of rare disorders that anyone would've ruled out after twenty years . . . why should I let you get close to a patient I've sealed off from the rest of the staff? And please, assume my reasons are *intelligent* this time."

"I . . ." I paused to collect my thoughts. "I suppose it's pointless just to ask what those reasons actually are?"

"No, I'm glad you would ask," she said, and, to my surprise, she smiled. "Let's assume it's pointless for now, but I credit you for asking a question instead of rushing to try to answer this time. That's one mark in your favor. However, I'd like you to try to guess the answer, and if it's insightful enough, perhaps I'll tell you."

I considered. "Well, there are a couple of things that don't quite make sense about how he's treated. I'm going to assume those are by design, so let me see if I can start with that and work my way up."

She didn't say anything, but she also didn't stop smiling. I was either on the right track or so spectacularly wrong it was funny.

"Let's start with the fact that you tell me anyone can talk to him if they want to, but nobody actually does," I said. "And yet, I told Dr. P—— I wanted to attempt therapy with Joe and he flipped out. Theoretically, therapy can involve nothing *but* talking to someone, but if anyone's allowed to talk to him, then that must mean that you think he needs something other than talk therapy and medicine, or at least on top of that. Something that requires hospital resources beyond just a doctor's time and prescription pad."

"You're on the wrong track," she said, with a slight shake of her head. Fighting the urge to wince, I started again.

"All right, so maybe you don't need more than just talk therapy and medicine to treat him," I began, speaking more slowly this time as I tried to work out the puzzle. "And anyway, you still discourage talking to him so heavily that I'm betting there's something dangerous about doing as little as that. But even if he's fine in small doses, randomly talking to a patient doesn't mean therapy. I can walk up to a catatonic patient and start talking to him, but that doesn't make him *my* patient. I'm not responsible for him just because I've tried talking to him. But if I formally take him on as a patient, then I've got a lot more responsibility both for his treatment and for making sure it doesn't go wrong. Maybe his family could sue us if we did something really wrong. *On the other hand . . .*"

She was starting to interrupt, which meant that my last four words probably sounded more panicky than they should have, but they had the desired effect. She shut her mouth and continued listening. I exhaled slowly.

"On the other hand," I continued, "you already think he's incurable, so I'm guessing other doctors have tried everything they can with him and he hasn't been removed from your custody yet, so worries about his family being dissatisfied must not be a factor. Which means there's someone else you're protecting."

All at once, a bolt of realization struck me. "There must be! Because there's a note in his file from the last medical director to *you* saying that even if his family stopped paying, he should be kept here at the hospital's expense in order to protect the outside world from him. But that still doesn't explain why you'd be so anxious about preventing doctors from taking him on as a patient. We're supposed to handle things that most people can't."

Words were tumbling out now, and I doubt she could have stopped me if she'd wanted to. But she showed no sign of wanting to. If anything, she looked almost proud.

"Unless the problem is even *more* dangerous for us," I went on. "Which isn't a normal problem to have with a psych patient, but it's pretty normal if you're dealing with someone who's under quarantine for a highly contagious disease. Those patients really *are* kept off-limits except to people who follow the proper procedures for treating them safely because of the increased risk from prolonged exposure. Just being in the same room as an Ebola patient for a few minutes doesn't guarantee you'll get infected, but spending hours trying to treat them without proper procedures is practically a death sentence.

"Similarly, judging by the way you've set everything up, talking to this patient for a few minutes probably doesn't put anyone in danger. But I saw what

happened to Graham, the orderly, and to Nessie. She was exposed to him every night and ended up committing suicide. Which means you're worried about us taking him on as a patient because it means prolonged exposure, which puts us more at risk of his driving us to do something like what she did."

I stopped suddenly and felt a creeping chill run over me. "Dr. G—, if there were others who treated him . . . um . . . can I ask what happened to them?"

She lifted her hands and clapped slowly. "Now *that's* a question I can answer." She spoke softly. Her voice was no longer sharp, but instead mournful. "For that, you'll have to come with me."

She got up and left Dr. P—'s office at a brisk pace, not checking to see if I was following. I hustled out and caught up to her at the elevator. We rode in silence up to the top floor, then went into her office. After unlocking a drawer, she pulled out a thick manila file and opened it.

"Dr. A— obviously did the initial diagnosis, or attempted it, anyway," she said. "But you probably noticed the four-year gap after that. Well, believe it or not, we didn't leave Joe completely alone during that time. People did try to treat him. In fact . . ."

She swallowed hard. "I was the first. I'd just started at the hospital myself, and Dr. A— sent me to try it. I'd graduated at the top of my class, performed with excellence at my residency and fellowship, and psy-

chiatric hospitals were better funded in those days, so they could afford the cream of the crop. You aren't the only one often accused of being the smartest person in the room."

She glanced to her right, and I looked up and saw her degrees. MD and PhD. *Veritas.* Plus her residency at the best hospital in the country, a fellowship, and two separate board certifications. She was quite a diplomate.

"Dr. A— was right. I was the smartest person in the room. But that didn't stop me from trying to swallow a bottle of pills from the nurse's office just four months into treating Joe. After that, Dr. A— removed me and placed me on mandatory paid psychological leave so that I could get therapy to recover from the experience. I spent a few more months in a private clinic before returning, and I was never assigned to interact with Joe again. After me, his next doctor spent a year trying to treat him. That ended when the doctor in question stopped showing up for work. He was found two days later when we filed a missing person's report. The police discovered him hiding in his house, suffering from what I gather must've been the aftereffects of a psychotic break. I say 'I gather' because the instant they entered his house, he ran at them with a knife, giving them no choice but to shoot him to death."

She paused, gave me a significant look, and went on. "Joe's next doctor lasted only six months before she went catatonic and had to be institutionalized here. I would say you might have treated her without knowing it, only she somehow managed to get hold of something sharp and slit her throat with it about a month before you started. In any case, after her, we assigned someone a bit tougher to work on Joe's case. He had a military background and came to us from a hospital where he'd focused on the criminally insane. He lasted eighteen months before he sent us a one-sentence resignation letter and put a bullet through his brain."

She reached the end of the page and heaved a very deep sigh. "After that, Thomas, Dr. A—, I mean, decided to take on the case himself. And to his credit, he actually survived the experience. However, he still stopped treatment after eight months. And before he resigned as medical director a few years later, he joined the board so he could make sure every future medical director after him would sign an agreement promising not to assign anyone to Joe's case without personally interviewing each one for suitability first. Like all my predecessors, I have complied and refused to assign Joe a doctor without one of these screenings. Because you're right. His madness is contagious. I've seen it destroy my colleagues and even the man who mentored and groomed me for the job I hold today. And it almost destroyed me."

Her eyes met mine, and for a moment, I saw something behind the cold, sharp woman she'd been. I saw a crushed, angry young doctor who'd thought she was brilliant, just as I did, and who had been able only to watch helplessly as one patient ruined her life and the lives of those around her.

"You're screening me," I said softly. She nodded.

"What does he do to people, Dr. G——? If his madness is so contagious, I'd like to know what I should be afraid of. Maybe I can guard against it."

Her eyebrows shot up, and a bitter smile settled onto her lips.

"I'm afraid I can't answer that, Parker," she said. "Unfortunately, that's a question only you can answer, and you've earned the right, much as I hate the idea of putting anyone else in danger. But you've shown enough brains to suggest that maybe you might be able to do something with him. So let me ask you—what do you fear most?"

"Um." I tried to think, but nothing came to mind. "I . . . I don't know?"

"Sorry, that won't do," she said. "If you're going to attempt therapy with him, you need to know the answer to that question before you do. It's your first line of defense. In fact, if you treat him, it's mine, too, because if I don't know the answer to that question, I'll have no idea what might be stalking my ward after your first therapy session with him. Try again. Take your time."

An acute chill ran up my back. "You mean he can just tell whatever—"

"Just. Answer. The question."

That was as close to a yes as it could get. So I thought. I thought for several minutes, in complete silence, with Dr. G—— never doing anything to interrupt me. She seemed as fascinated by the answer to come as I was stumped. I thought of all the usual answers, of course—drowning, insects, fire—but one thing kept forcing itself back into my mind: the image of my mother in her hospital room. There was only one answer I could give.

"I'm most afraid of not being able to protect the people I care about," I said finally. "I'm most afraid of being helpless to save someone."

Dr. G—— raised her eyebrows in genuine surprise.

"Interesting," she said. "And just now, is there anyone on my staff you care about so much that it would hurt you if they dropped dead? Don't bother being polite."

Feeling chagrined despite her last instruction, I shook my head. She nodded.

"I thought not. You haven't been here long enough, really," she said. "See that you don't develop any such attachments anytime soon." Without saying anything else, she pulled a blank sheet of paper from her desk, scribbled something on it, signed her name, and handed it to me.

"Take this to Dr. P——. As of now, you are Joe's new doctor," she said. "I will reassign you if you ask me to, on one condition. You must make an appointment with me and tell me, in the most exacting detail you can provide, what he did that made you decide you were not fit to continue as his physician." She reached into her drawer, pulled out the two audiotapes, and shoved them into my hands along with the missing patient file.

"Oh, and Parker? Try not to kill yourself first," she said, meeting my eyes. "Now, find Bruce, wherever he's sulking, and give him that note."

I found Dr. P—— sitting in one of the ward's lobby chairs, looking both mutinous and terribly tired. As I approached his chair, he gave a dissatisfied grunt by way of acknowledgment but didn't turn around.

"What is it, wonder boy?" he asked. "You all done with your heart-to-heart with the boss? Here to clean out your desk?"

I didn't know how to react, so I just pushed the note over his shoulder. He took it, read it, and slumped over in his chair like a man who'd just gotten word that a close relative had been murdered. Then he turned to look at me, and for the first time, his expression was neither hostile nor angry. Instead, his eyes held only defeat and fear.

"Well, I'll be damned," he breathed. "Rose must think you're as smart as you do. Too bad. Because I know that you trying this makes you the dumbest and craziest motherfucker on this ward. Well, now we'll find out exactly how dumb. Just make sure you don't let your shiny new freak make you fall behind in your other duties. I expect you to hold to all parts of your proposal."

I nodded. "Of course. Is there anything else you wanted to talk about with my proposed new patient list and intake hours?"

He gave a hollow laugh. "No, kid, no, I don't. Now stop wasting my time and go do something for your new charges. Even Joe."

He flashed me a wry, humorless smile. "I'm guessing you don't need help finding his room?"

No. I didn't.

March 24, 2008

Whew. All right, this one I have to write quickly, otherwise I'll never finish it. Gonna have a killer hangover, but fuck it. Getting this stuff down on paper is like chemotherapy for my soul. It fucking hurts, but it's burning something worse out. No point putting it off either way, so let's talk about my first meeting with Joe. And, yes, I've tried to write this exactly as I remember it, but I obviously didn't have a tape recorder with me, so if I have to paraphrase a bit in places just so it doesn't sound disjointed, I trust you'll cut me some slack.

Although its occupant was so feared and despised by the rest of the hospital staff, Joe's room fulfilled very few horror clichés. True, it was at the end of a long hallway, giving anyone who was walking toward it plenty of time to reflect on what they were doing with presumably mounting dread, but I'm sure this was deliberate. Considering the contents of even his abridged file, keeping Joe so far away from other patients made sense, and since very few members of staff interacted with him, that was all the more reason to put him out of the way. And given the reference in his file to his family's wealth, perhaps it was also an act of deference to them to give him one of the more spacious and well-lit rooms in the hospital, despite the frequent shortage of beds and space.

Even so, if you think any of that diminished my apprehension when I took those first few steps down the hallway, you are gravely mistaken. Until this point, Joe had been only a distant intellectual puzzle, to be imagined and theorized over. But now I was officially his doctor. And although perhaps it was too late for common sense, I suddenly felt more than a little jittery about my first meeting with a patient whose death toll extended not only to other patients but even to those trained to face insanity without fear. The words of Dr. G—, Dr. P—, and, most of all, Nessie kept echoing through my head. By the time I reached his door, I half expected it to shock me when I inserted my staff key and pulled the knob. But nothing of the sort happened.

For such a formidable patient, Joe did not give even the slightest impression of danger. He couldn't have been more than five feet six and was about as thin as one could get without appearing underfed. A mop of unruly blond hair that looked as if it hadn't been combed in years flopped around his face.

He was sitting with his back to me in one of the cheap hospital chairs, and as he stood up and turned, I expected his face to carry some sort of unexpected terror. But even here, I was disappointed. His face was long, pale, and horsey, with a weak, drooping chin, high cheekbones, and slightly yellowed teeth. His pale blue eyes looked unfocused and almost as absent as those of some of the more catatonic patients I'd seen.

We stood staring at each other for a few moments before I spoke.

"Joe?" I said in my most professional tones. "I'm Dr. H——. Dr. G—— assigned me to do therapy with you, if that's all right with you."

He didn't say anything. He didn't react at all.

"If this is a bad time, I can come—"

"You're young."

His voice was reedy and low, and rasped as if he barely used it. It would have been slightly disconcerting if not for the thick sorrow in it, which only made him seem more pathetic.

I nodded at him and gave him a small smile. "I am," I said calmly. "Does that bother you?"

He shrugged. "The others weren't as young as you. Should I be impressed?"

I blinked. "Impressed? By what?"

"Well, you must've *really* pissed someone off to get sent in here at your age."

Without thinking, I smiled. I had braced myself for the worst when I entered this room. I had expected verbal abuse, taunting, recitations of disturbing fantasies, and possibly even attempts to act on them. The one thing I hadn't expected was for Joe to crack a joke, let alone actually be *funny*.

"You might be right about that, but why would that impress you?"

Joe shrugged. "I'm impressed with anyone who irritates the staff here. To me, that makes you a kindred soul. Besides, whatever you did to make them give you *me* as a patient must've been *really* fucking bad."

His expression soured. "That, or *she's* gotten even meaner in her old age. Or desperate."

"Who?"

"You know who," he said with a bitter smile. "Her. The one who keeps me locked up here. Why doesn't she just cut my throat while she's at it? I'd wager she's done it to plenty of others."

"If you're referring to Dr. G—, I—"

"Oh, doctor, doctor, doctor," Joe said softly. Then, without warning, he smacked the wall and gave a disgusted snort. "Well, she's a shit doctor. Can't heal a patient, so she locks me up with barely anyone to talk to for decades, then sends in a fresh face like you. Let me guess. You're the brightest new doctor on the block, and they think maybe you, and only you, could heal me?"

I shouldn't have been surprised that he'd worked out what I'd thought were private details about me, but I was. My shock must've shown in my face, because he chuckled disdainfully.

"It's not like I had to be magic to figure it out," he said. "That bitch would send someone in here for only one reason: Because she wants to fire them. You know I was probably in here when you were in diapers, and no one since then has had any idea what to do with me? She knows I'm not 'curable,' you realize. You're just a sacrificial lamb who'll give her something to report to my worthless fucking parents so they'll keep sending money, and she can get rid of any bright, fresh faces who might make her look bad."

I was shocked. This wasn't at all how I'd imagined the most feared patient in the hospital would act. He was bitter and frustrated, yes, but seemed remarkably lucid, even sane. Hardly fruit for twenty-plus years of confusion and terror, let alone remaining in hospital custody. What was more, his comments left a bad taste in my mouth and made me doubt what I'd been told. Could all the stories about him really be just an elaborate act to maintain such a reliable revenue stream for the hospital? I quirked an eyebrow.

"Joe, you don't think there's anything wrong with you?"

"How the fuck should I know?" Joe shot back. "As far as I can tell, it's everyone else who goes insane around me! It's happened so often I sometimes wonder if they're doing it on purpose, just to make me go as fucking nuts as they are from anticipating what crazy-shit thing someone will do next."

He sounded too sincere to be lying, and despite everything I'd learned, I began to feel sorry for him. Still, some of the stories I'd heard had stuck with me enough to make me wary, so I didn't reply immediately. Better to keep him talking.

"Well, go ahead, get it over with," he said with a bitter laugh. "I'm sure I've done something to drive you nuts without realizing it in the past few minutes."

I shook my head. "No."

"Well, glory halle-fucking-lujah. But I can see the gears turning in that bright young brain of yours. Go on, spit it out. What's got you scrunching up your face like that?"

I shrugged. "Honestly, I don't know what to think, Joe. You don't seem like a monster, but your file does have some troubling stuff in it."

"Oh yeah?" he sneered. "This should be good. Like what?"

"Well," I said, "I don't think a normal person would try to rape a six-year-old boy on his first night sharing a room with him."

Joe snorted. "Is that what the file says happened with Nathan?"

I had to repress a double take. Someone as remorselessly evil as Joe had been made out to be didn't usually remember individual victims by name after this much time. They might remember the acts, but generally the victims were so dehumanized in their minds that names weren't part of the package.

"What did happen with Nathan, Joe?" I asked. "Why don't you give me your side of the story?"

He didn't answer at first but kicked back on his bed in disgust. After a few moments of silence, he gave me an appraising look.

"Before I tell you," he said, "I've just got one question for you."

"Yes?"

"Got any chewing gum?" He gave me an uneven grin. "I used to get it from Nessie. Keeps my mind occupied a bit. Relieves the boredom."

As it happens, I did have a very worn-out old pack of gum in one pocket. I scooped it out and handed him a stick. He took it, unwrapped it, and popped the whole thing into his mouth with obvious relish, then smiled crookedly at me again.

"Thanks, doc," he said. "I guess you might be all right."

I smiled back despite my confusion. "So . . . Nathan?"

"Right, Nathan." Joe chewed thoughtfully. "Well, I know this is what a lot of people say, but the thing is . . . he came on to me."

"I find that hard to believe, Joe. He was six. You were ten."

"Yeah yeah, I know, it's too young," Joe said angrily, waving my comment away as if it were a fly, "but do you think he knew that? His dad had been fucking him since he could walk. I think he just thought that was love. Anyway, he told me he couldn't sleep unless someone 'put it in him' first and asked me to do it. Well, I was a kid, and I didn't know any better. They don't exactly give you the birds-and-bees talk in a place like this, y'know. So I did. But because I didn't know what I was doing and didn't have anything to make it go in easier, he started screaming. The orderlies were right outside, so I couldn't exactly get off him. And do you think they were going to listen to me after what they thought they saw?"

He rolled his eyes. "I shouldn't complain, I guess, since at least I won't die a virgin. Not how I'd have chosen to lose it, but we can't have everything."

Although it went against my better judgment, I had to admit the story sounded plausible. Still, there was too much in that file for the contents to be nothing but misunderstandings. I pressed him further.

"Even if I believe you, Joe," I said, "it's not like that's the only thing. Your doctors keep dying or going nuts."

"And you think I'm doing it?" Joe asked. He waved at his body in exasperation. "Do I look threatening to you, doctor?"

"No," I said, "but if you're gaslighting them . . ."

"If I'm what?"

Right, he might not be as familiar with that term. It's doubtful anyone showed him the movie. "I mean, if you are deliberately trying to drive them insane."

He scoffed. "Bullshit. They didn't kill themselves because I was crazy. They killed themselves because they, and everyone who ever worked on my case, knew I was sane."

My jaw dropped before I could think to stop it. Seeing this, Joe guffawed.

"Oh, I know, I know, it sounds ridiculous, but you can believe me, it's true. Has been since the second time my asshole parents left me here to get me out of their hair 'cause they couldn't deal with me and told the doctors to come up with a reason to keep me. Well, like the greedy fucks they were, they made shit up, but at least they knew at first what a farce it all was. Before she came along."

He growled low in his throat and spat on the ground before continuing. "You know what I was going to be before your precious little Dr. G— worked here, doc? I was going to be the bitch case. That smug prick Dr. A— made it more or less official policy that only the lowest-ranking doctors would be assigned to work on me because no one wanted to do therapy with a sane patient who was being kept here purely at his parents' request. Chalk it up to my bad luck that Dr. G— was the first one to get that assignment. Because let me tell you, Dr. G—? She was too ambitious to waste her time with that. So what does she do? She spins a little tale about how terrifying I am to work with and leaves a suicide note about it just where the other doctors will find it, and next thing you know, she's on sick leave, gets to work with real patients when she comes back, and I go from being the case no one cares about to being the case no one dares to talk to. So what do they do? They start sending the doctors they want to fire to work on me, 'cause that would give them an excuse to get rid of those poor fuckers. And those doctors knew that if they failed to cure me, that bitch and her cold-fish mentor would make sure their careers were over, but as soon as they talked to me, they knew they couldn't possibly do it because there was nothing to cure. The ones who lasted the longest were the ones who were able to talk themselves into drawing a paycheck just to spite this place. The longer they could live with that, the longer they stuck around. And I had to watch the only people who cared about me even slightly lose their minds in the process."

I still had doubts, but for some reason, the more Joe talked, the more my heart went out to him. If I had to guess what made him so sympathetic I'd say it was his demeanor. I'm not really getting it across here, but even though he was technically defending himself, his voice still sounded hollow and resigned, like he knew that even if I believed him, it wouldn't help anything. Like he was just giving his defense on autopilot. And because there was so little hope in what he was saying, it made me more inclined to believe he was being honest. I should've recognized that this could just as easily be a psychopath's manipulation, in retrospect, but, given how thoroughly he'd caught me off guard and how inexperienced I was, I was probably far more impressionable than I should've been.

That being said, I wasn't a complete naïf. I knew that any patient who isn't completely deluded or catatonic can game a first impression. So for the next forty-five minutes, I tried to steer the conversation so as to see if Joe gave any signs of serious latent psychological disorders, signs only a professional would know how to spot. But here, too, I ran into a dead end. Joe showed no signs of any mental illness beyond mild depression and agoraphobia, both of which I would expect from a patient who'd been locked up for twenty-plus years facing doctors whose sanity was gradually deteriorating.

Granted, a very skilled psychopath could've faked all of this, but Joe gave none of the indicators that this was the case. For example, during our first talk, I recall that a bird flew into his window and stunned itself. A psychopath wouldn't have reacted at all, but Joe walked over to the window and watched in concern, his face pressed against the glass, until the bird shook itself and flew away. If there was a clearer sign of healthy empathy, I would've been hard put to imagine it.

The upshot of all this was that when I closed the door to Joe's room after that first meeting, I felt sick, though not for any of the reasons I had expected. The fact was that despite every horrifying story his file contained, I saw absolutely no evidence that this man was anything other than a desperately lonely scapegoat, abandoned by his parents and made into an underfunded, understaffed hospital's resident freak. Under the circumstances, I would ordinarily have recommended to my superior that he be released, but if even part of Joe's story was true, that obviously would've been a terrible decision. If he was right, then this hospital wasn't going to let a cash cow like him go, even if he was sane.

Then again, it was just one session, and the accusations against him were numerous. I decided I'd give myself a month of sessions with him before I decided to do anything drastic. Perhaps I'd simply caught him on a good day, and in a little while he'd transform into the nightmare-channeling fiend depicted in his file. Besides, I still hadn't listened to the audiotapes in his full file, nor had I looked at the unredacted notes from the attending physicians that Dr. G— had given me.

I shouldn't admit this, but I took his file home with me. If Dr. G— was keeping it locked in a drawer in her usually locked office, I didn't feel safe leaving it in mine. My battered institutional desk didn't lock, and I didn't have a reputation for securing my office because patient records going forward were all digitized and I didn't leave anything sensitive or valuable lying around.

When I got home, I couldn't immediately start reading. That night was a particularly hard one for Jocelyn and me. Between my new job, which included an obsession with Joe, and her frustration with her research, we hadn't had a lot of time together. I think that was the week she broke down and told me that her professor had trashed an entire year's worth of her writing. Mentors are supposed to support their grad students, but this one member of her committee was an intransigent asshole, constantly negging her and her work. I suspected he wanted to sleep with her or, at the least, felt threatened by her. Or maybe this was just his idea of normal, since a lot of apprenticeship programs have weird traditions of abuse that everyone has to get through, a way of "paying their dues." We had a fight, but it was short-lived. She got me to talk about the nightmare I'd had that had woken her, and I got her to share her problems with her professor. We were so tired in the end that we fell asleep curled together, our respective work put away for a night.

I didn't get started on Joe's material 'til the following night, and I decided to begin with the audiotapes. My thought was that the first session with Joe—when he ostensibly was suffering only from night terrors—might give me some clues that other doctors had missed because of its seeming banality.

The audiotape of Joe's first session was old and more than a little warped, and I was worried that it wouldn't work when I popped it into my cassette tape player. However, after a few disconcerting grinding and whirring noises, the cassette's spools began to turn, and the tinny sound of a man's voice, tinged with a mid-Atlantic accent, flowed from my speakers.

> `Hello, Joe, my name is Dr. A—. Your parents tell me you have trouble sleeping.`

There was a brief interval in which I imagined Joe must have nodded, because Dr. A— went on speaking.

> `Could you tell me why that is?`

Another brief pause, then a child's voice answered.

The thing in my walls won't let me.

A: I see. I'm sorry to hear that. Could you tell me about the thing in your walls?

J: It's gross.

A: Gross? How so?

J: Just gross. And scary.

A: What I mean is, can you describe it?

J: It's big and hairy. It's got fly eyes and two big, superstrong spider arms with really long fingers. Its body is a worm.

I let out an involuntary shudder. Even for an imaginative kid, that was a pretty ugly mental image. Even so, Joe had been listed as an acute entomophobe, so this seemed like a natural expression of that fear. No reason so far to think he was anything more than a typical fearful child. Dr. A— had apparently felt the same way.

A: That does sound scary. And how big is it?

J: Big! Bigger than daddy's car!

A: I see. And have your parents ever seen it?

J: No. It goes back in the walls when they come.

A: Something that big can fit in your walls? They don't break?

J: It melts. Like ice cream. It looks like it is the wall.

A: I see. And it's what made those marks on your arms?

J: Yes. I tried covering my face so I wouldn't have to see it. It pulled my arms away and made me open my eyes with its fingers.

A: Why did it do that?

J: It likes when I feel bad. That's why it doesn't let me sleep.

A: What do you mean?

J: It eats bad thoughts.

Yeesh. If he hadn't been locked in the hospital, this kid would've made a great horror author.

He was also—to my deep frustration—completely ordinary. As I continued to listen, I cracked a smile at what a brave kid he was. I could also see that the information on the tape largely conformed to the notes in the file, and nothing in the session suggested anything like the horrors that this little boy had visited on the hospital after his second admission. In fact, based only on the tape, everything that followed this session seemed impossible. Something about this story just didn't add up, which gave me an unpleasant thrill of suspicion that what the adult Joe had told me about being set up might actually be true.

Even so, this was just one set of data. To try to understand what Joe had evidently become while in captivity, I would need to turn to the second tape, the one produced by the orderly who'd stayed one night with him.

On first looking at it, I did notice something that seemed odd. A narrow strip of what looked like very old masking tape with the words "3 a.m.–4 a.m." written on it had been stuck to the cassette. I was puzzled. Why record only one hour? Then it hit me. The file mentioned that the recording had been mostly silent. This must be the only tape that contained anything of interest. Otherwise, why preserve it? Prepping myself to listen very hard for something over the next hour, I pushed the cassette in and pressed Play.

It was, as I suspected, almost nothing but dead air for the first twenty minutes, and more than once, I had to stop myself from zoning out. Eventually, I resorted to counting the seconds under my breath, periodically looking at my watch as a means of making sure I stayed attentive to *something*. When I reached the twenty-minute mark, the tape seemed to come to life, and I did hear something.

First, there was the sound of breathing that I'd seen mentioned in the file. Dr. A— hadn't exaggerated: this was undoubtedly the sound of someone having an anxiety attack. The breathing went on for about thirty seconds before I heard the sound of something shifting and then . . .

Footsteps. Fast footsteps, as if someone was running, followed by the smack of something soft on something hard. Throughout, I heard heavy breathing, presumably of the person who'd just been running, then a rough voice muttering several obscene words over and over again in increasingly terrified accents. Next, there was the sound of shuffling footsteps, and abruptly, at thirty minutes, the recording seemed to completely cut off.

Annoyed, I rewound it. It was obvious what I had heard. The orderly had clearly been too freaked out to stay the whole night and had made a run for it—that is, assuming the notes were accurate. He might have just decided to go home and faked the scares to keep the legend of Joe alive. However, just to be sure, I thought I should listen to the ten minutes of activity again, to make sure I hadn't misheard. This time, I pulled out a set of headphones, plugged them into the cassette player, and turned the volume up as high as it would go without hurting my ears.

Again, the same sounds. The rapid-fire, anxious breathing. The sound of a shifting body. The running footsteps. The swearing. The laughter. The shuffling walk away.

Hang on. *Laughter?* That hadn't been there before. I rewound the tape again and listened.

At a lower volume, the sound easily could've been mistaken for background noise. But through headphones cranked up that high, it was indubitable. While the orderly swore into his mic, I thought I could hear, in the gaps between his epithets, the sound of a low, rumbling chuckle in the background, as if it were being recorded from a great distance. But even from a distance, I could tell that the sound must have been far louder in person to have been picked up by the mic. If not for the poor quality of the recording, which made me doubt its accuracy, I'd probably have been freaked out enough to drop the case right there.

You see, that laugh did not sound like any sound a person should be able to produce. It was too hoarse, too low, and too guttural, almost as if someone had given the rhythm of a human laugh to the sound of a glacier collapsing. But then, it was far away, and the recording was very old, so for all I knew, it was just something innocuous in the background that had gotten warped over years of disuse. I ejected the tape, figuring there was nothing else I could learn from it, and settled down to have a look at the notes.

These I will not bother transcribing, and for this reason: If I'd thought before reading them that Joe was mistaken about being given the worst doctors in the hospital, I was convinced he was correct afterwards. These were some of the most disjointed, unhelpful, and frankly incoherent notes I'd read in my life. They jumped from diagnosis to diagnosis, and medication to medication, seemingly turning on a dime, until I began to wonder if Joe might have simply been slowly driven insane by the many different side effects. Some made reference to having him restrained, or even muzzled, including during talk therapy sessions, which seemed completely counterproductive to me. I mean, what's the point of talk therapy if the patient can't speak? Suffice it to say, by the end, I was all but certain that these people were just taking out their frustrations with their own medical ineptitude on a helpless patient, and I shuddered to think how many malpractice lawsuits could've been filed on the basis of what I'd read.

The only notes I could even begin to follow were the ones written by Dr. G——, and while they did show a highly competent physician at work, at the end of the day, they all but confirmed Joe's hypothesis. Dr. G——'s notes were very dismissive at first, and I could practically hear the resentment in every sentence she wrote about him. It was obvious that she thought this patient was entirely beneath her and she wanted desperately to be reassigned. Yet as the notes went on, the resentment seemed to bleed out of her tone and give way to an extreme sense of triumph.

At the same time, they got shorter and shorter, as if she was becoming more and more certain that she wouldn't need notes because the case was so close to being resolved. This is a good example:

```
Joe responding well to final treatment.
Will check back in a week, if the pro-
cess even takes that long to work.
```

Well, whatever "final treatment" she referred to definitely had borne *some* sort of results. You see, exactly a week later, that brief, almost flippant aside was followed by her final memo, which was so different it was almost whiplash-inducing. That memo I will transcribe here.

Effective tomorrow, I am resigning my post at CSA. I have failed my patients, failed my colleagues, and failed myself. Nothing can ever make up for it. Please do not bother sending my last paycheck, as I don't deserve it and don't expect to need it. Thank you for the opportunity to work with you, and I am sorry I let you down so thoroughly. I am sorry. So so sorry.

—*Rose*

Needless to say, this seemed suspicious. True, Dr. G—— could've merely picked a disastrously wrong final treatment, but in view of what I'd read and heard, it seemed far more likely that she'd intended only that it would be the final treatment *she* would provide for Joe because she planned to fake a suicide attempt. Otherwise, why would her notes be so short on details about her seemingly successful treatment?

This, from my perspective, was almost the final nail in the "mystery patient no one can cure" theory's coffin. Though I still resolved to give Joe a month's worth of observation, I was already beginning to wonder what it would take to prove to some higher authority in the world of medicine just how much abuse this one poor man had suffered at the hands of the unethical and callous Dr. G——. If I'd thought I might have overlooked something when I'd heard the phantom laughter on the tape earlier, I now wondered if the tape had somehow been altered, since Dr. G—— had been the one holding on to it. Either way, from where I sat, it was Joe who'd been living in a nightmare, not his orderlies, and not his doctors.

No wonder Dr. P—— had snarled at me when I suggested taking Joe on as a patient. In fact, small wonder that Dr. P—— still had a position as a doctor, let alone a supervisory one, at all. He hadn't been put in charge of that ward to heal anyone; he'd been put there to act as a jailer for the hospital's one reliable revenue stream. He demonstrated his lack of empathy every time he skipped a meeting or told me to "just medicate them 'til they are numb." Of *course* it irritated him that someone like me had showed up on his ward looking to help people. That very impulse was a threat to the means by which he kept his job secure. Less well-qualified doctors who *needed* a job on his ward, rather than being there by choice, could be cowed by threats to their employment, but my pedigree put me out of reach, which must have galled that overgrown bully even more than the fact that someone with similar qualifications had leap-frogged over him in the race to be medical director. And to think he'd tried to pretend he was helping me by keeping me away from Joe. Bullshit. The old bastard had been trying to save himself.

Worse still, the whole affair cast Nessie's suicide in an entirely new light: That kindly old woman must've known what was going on. How could she not, having been Joe's nurse since he was a child? He was probably the closest thing to a son she'd had, and yet there she was, being asked to torture him with medication, captivity, and gaslighting for more than three decades. It was no surprise that she didn't want anyone else working on him; she must have thought she was the only one who would even think of being kind to him. And maybe Dr. G— and Dr. P— let her go on doing it because they thought she couldn't tear herself away from the hospital that had been her home for so long. But it appeared to have been too much even for her, and she'd killed herself out of guilt. Which explained why she tried to warn everyone, even people she trusted, away from Joe so they wouldn't have to suffer the same guilt.

And all because one cruel woman had been simply too arrogant and too ambitious to handle being given a dud case for her first assignment.

Even so, on some level, I felt relieved. This was a horror story all right, but at least it seemed like it probably had a human monster. And if Dr. G— was the monster I suspected, then I vowed that by the time this was over, I was going to put a stake through her heart.

March 27, 2008

All right, if you all have read this far, you don't need me to treat you with kid gloves and summarize where we are. You know we left off with me having my first session with a supposedly incurable patient, only to discover that he might actually be sane. Let's move on, and quickly.

Going back to the hospital the next day was, as you might expect, a fairly tense experience. Now that I was beginning to suspect that I would have to openly defy the medical director herself at my first real job after so many years of training, much of what had been routine suddenly seemed sinister. I studied the behavior of the various therapists in our morning-team patient care meeting. I reconsidered every new prescription I had thought to write, wondering if I was going to be scapegoated for any negative reactions. I watched the nurses rotating through their duties.

Once I started looking for patterns, it became excruciatingly obvious that I was being followed by two orderlies, the titans of the hospital. One, Marvin, was a baldheaded, pale behemoth at least six feet five inches tall whose hospital uniform stretched across his expansive chest and his tattoo-sleeved arms. The other, Hank, was a dreadlocked black colossus who was almost as vast as Marvin was tall and looked like he could squat twice his weight without breaking a sweat. They would've been noticeable even to an unobservant person, but to me, their constant lurking presence screamed malevolence. Not that they were obvious in their reconnaissance. No, they had enough wits to appear to be working whenever I spied them, whether it was checking a patient's chart or carrying mountains of supplies into the closets. In the beginning, it was only disquieting, but over the following days, I found myself deeply unsettled. Dr. G— had appeared positive about my taking on Joe, so putting me under surveillance seemed contrary and left me suspicious of her.

OK, so back to my treatment for Joe. Psychodynamic therapy, or talk therapy, as we often call it, usually involves one to two visits per week. At this point, I was concerned about getting a head start with him and covering a lot of background quickly. With my heavier workload, I had a lot to balance, but as I was coming off my residency—everyone knows doctors are sleep-deprived and overworked in those early years—I was up to handling it. All of which is to say, I was right back in his room for another session the day after I listened to those tapes.

I found Joe lounging on his bed, a half-finished game of solitaire in front of him. I have to admit, I was relieved to see this. If he was as sane as he claimed, it would have been cruel even for the most unethical doctors not to give him *some* form of entertainment.

He was looking at me with the same crooked grin he'd worn the previous day. "Hey there, doc," he said. "Nice seeing you again. I guess I didn't scare you off the first time after all."

I gave him a polite smile. "Hello, Joe."

Joe pulled himself into a cross-legged position on his bed and pointed to a folding chair in the corner. "Well, don't stand on my account. Sit down."

I pulled the chair into the center of the room, facing Joe, and made myself comfortable. "So, I read your full file last night."

"Oh yeah?" He raised his eyebrows. "And? How much of a dangerous nutcase do they say I am?"

"I think you know the answer to that, Joe."

His expression darkened. "Yeah, I do. The question is, do you believe it?"

"I don't know what to believe. I can tell your previous doctors weren't exactly paragons of medical efficacy, but there's much that just doesn't make sense."

"Oh yeah? Well, I've got all day, doc," Joe said quietly, before reaching down and shifting a few cards from pile to pile. "Why don't you ask away?"

"OK," I said. "Say you're telling the truth. Say you are being kept here just so the hospital can keep billing your parents. Your parents really wouldn't care if they knew that?"

Joe snorted. "Of course they wouldn't. My parents are very rich and only cared about me when I made them look good by being the perfect little boy. Once they figured out I wasn't like them, they probably thought locking me away here was worth it just to keep the neighbors from talking."

"What makes you so sure?" I asked. "Isn't it *possible* they just don't know you're being kept as a revenue stream for the hospital? That they believe you really need help?"

Joe's laugh was harsh. "Don't be an idiot. They wouldn't care either way."

"What makes you say that?"

Joe, who was in the middle of shifting cards between piles again, stopped and glared up at me. His voice was level, and yet every syllable was pregnant with hurt. "If my parents gave a shit about me, why haven't they visited me?"

I kept my expression bland, so as not to antagonize him or seem to be taking the bait. "Everyone's encouraged to stay away from you, Joe, even the doctors. It's not a stretch to think they might believe the same things we're told."

"It's not like I'm asking for them to waltz in with a knitted sweater every Christmas. But who said they couldn't at least come to look in through the window in my door once in nearly thirty fucking years? Or check to see who's treating me? None of the doctors I've had in this hellhole have ever mentioned them asking about me. I've asked the few people who come in here, orderlies and whatnot, directly, and they've all said no one from the outside comes looking for me. Face it, doc, they left me here to rot. They don't care where I am, so long as it's not with them."

I must not have looked sufficiently convinced or else I'd touched a nerve, because his frustration gathered energy. "Let me tell you a story, doc, and you'll see what heartless shitheels my parents are.

"When I was five, just a year before they decided to get rid of me, I met a stray cat out in the woods on my family's estate. But she wasn't like just any stray cat. She was friendly and tame and would let me pet her and even hold her. I called her Fiberwood Flower, or Fiber for short, because my dad had made his fortune in textiles, so I used to hear him use the phrase 'fiberwood.' And she was pretty, so calling her a flower seemed appropriate. I was a kid, y'know, so just mixing words together seemed fine. Well, eventually, she stopped hiding in the woods and started coming onto my family's estate to visit me. I'd leave out scraps for her, from food I didn't eat, and we sort of got close. That is, until my parents found out."

His fist clenched. "My dad was allergic to cats. And as soon as he knew I'd been sneaking one onto the estate, he was furious. I tried to tell them I'd be good and wouldn't let her upset him, and that she was a nice cat, and my friend, but my dad didn't care. He marched right out of the house over to where Fiber was sitting. Well, she was used to people being friendly, so of course she didn't run. I wish she had, though. Because when he got to her, he picked her up and *dropkicked her into the fucking woods* before telling me if I ever got near her again, he'd do the same to me. Then he took a switch to me before he locked me in my room. I never saw her again." He paused, looking down at the cards. Then he raised his head and gazed at me. "Oh, and you are probably wondering where my mother was while I was screaming and crying in the garden having my naked back whipped."

He paused. Whatever his hesitation, he seemed uncomfortable with what he was about to share.

"My mother was telling my dad to stop because, she said, 'the neighbors might hear.' And my dad rounded on her. 'The neighbors will talk? Joseph snuck a cat onto our property, Martha. A fucking cat. You know what I get like around them. You want me to die, Martha? You want me to fucking die just so the neighbors won't talk?' Then he hit her in the face so hard she fell over. She never stood up to him again after that. And even though the beating I got was bad, seeing her with her eye swollen and black-and-blue for the next week or so was worse. Every time I think about why I'm here, I remember her walking around with her eye like that. I think she blamed me, and frankly, I kinda blame myself for being so stupid. I still dream of her glaring at me through that black eye, and sometimes when I wake up, I think my being here is punishment for putting my mom through that. I know, it's a dumb thing to think, but when you're a kid desperate to be loved, you'll believe anything is your fault if it'll make your parents love you again. Too bad that's impossible for me."

It was a stomach-churning story. I kept my eyes level with his and said, "I believe you."

And Joe's expression altered startlingly; he looked up at me with a smile that radiated relief.

April 3, 2008

So don't take this the wrong way, but I've never seen so many comments that both call me stupid *and* beg me for more information in the same place. Mixed signals, eh? Nah, I get it. This story is pretty damn cinematic, and I guess your comments about my judgment just reflect how much you're into the story. You sound like a horror film audience yelling at the babysitter not to go down into the basement! Well, too bad, what's done is done. Here's what happened next.

The sympathy I felt for Joe after hearing his heart-wrenching story stayed with me long after I exited his room on that fateful second day of our interactions. In fact, it permanently affected how I related to my job. Where once I had seen my decision to work at CSA as merely an abstract attempt to save patients who were considered disposable, as my mother once had been, now my decision to stay became acutely personal. Joe needed me, either to prove he was sane, as I now thought was almost certainly the case, or to root out whatever traces of latent insanity had lodged themselves in the brain of this lonely, abused pariah. Yes, even the most kind-hearted doctor has a duty to treat the utterances of mental patients with some degree of skepticism, but the sheer clarity and emotional honesty in Joe's description of the incident with Fiberwood Flower, the cat, suggested that it was either a very, very well-constructed delusion—which didn't preclude it from bearing some tenuous connection to reality—or a genuine memory. Either way, I saw it as a signpost that might help me begin to plumb the depths of Joe's mind.

Moreover, the story gave me a game plan for the month that I would spend evaluating Joe and determining whether or not I believed his story. Even if I couldn't treat him for the fantastic disorders attributed to him in his file, he had other issues I could address. He was obviously suffering from depression, for example, and with good reason, and the abuse from his parents, not to mention whatever else had happened, had clearly made it difficult for him to trust people.

This obviously necessitated going back to look at his file, albeit with a more skeptical eye. While most of it now seemed to be a fabrication, I did notice a couple of details that whoever had written the reports hadn't bothered to disguise. Perhaps most important was the fact that Joe had been committed by his guardians, which meant that, theoretically, since he was well over eighteen now, he should have been able to check himself out. I resolved to broach this at the next meeting we had.

Big mistake.

"Why not just walk out?" I asked as Joe and I played cards in his room during our second week of sessions. "If your parents really don't care where you are, why not leave? You are considered a voluntary committal, and now you are legally an adult. You can leave against medical advice."

"Did you even read my file?" he asked softly. The temperature in the room suddenly felt arctic.

"Yes. All of it. Why—"

"Then why are you asking me a question you know the answer to?"

"I . . . I'm not," I said slowly. "Joe, if there's something keeping you here, I don't know anything about it."

He sighed deeply. "I've been *trying* to leave since I turned eighteen. But who'd let me out if they saw what was in my file? Used to be they'd send in a new doctor every couple of years just to keep the trick going, and when the doctors got too scared, they started making shit up. Fuck. Gum, please."

I had taken to carrying gum with me, since I expected he would want some when we met. I pulled out a stick and watched him furiously munch on it. Seeming a bit pacified, he went on.

"I almost thought I might get out back when Nessie was giving me my meds every night."

I stared. "Nessie?" I asked, my mouth dry. "What did Nessie have to do with it?"

The look he gave me was laced with pity.

"So you knew Nessie," he said sorrowfully. "Well, then tell me something, doc. Does Nessie seem the type to be a good jailer?"

I didn't have to think about it. I shook my head. He smiled mournfully.

"Well, you're right. She wasn't," he said. "She knew what they were doing, and it was killing her inside. At the same time, even I knew they couldn't fire her, and she didn't want to leave. It's only because she was so attached to this place that I couldn't get her to agree to spill the beans. That is, until the last night I saw her. You know, the one when she 'committed suicide'?"

"You don't mean to say . . ."

"That they killed her over it? No, I don't," he said. "Because I couldn't prove it even if I did mean to say it. All the same, if I had any illusions about getting out, they died right before you showed up."

The psychiatrist part of my brain screamed at me that this must be a product of Joe's isolation, which might well have made him paranoid, even delusional about the prospect of escape. If it had been any other patient, that's exactly what I would have told myself and not lost any sleep over it. But this case was already so strange that this explanation seemed almost laughably insufficient. Joe seemed so lucid about everything else that it was very difficult to imagine a delusion like this being buried beneath that façade. Besides, if it was a delusion, how to explain Nessie's death? I'd seen her very shortly before her death. She had appeared tired, and unsure of herself, yes, but that was a long way from suicidal ideation. And anyway, on the off chance that Joe wasn't paranoid, this would go well beyond the realm of medical malpractice, and into serious criminal conspiracy. I was frightened of what might happen if I tried to interfere, but I was even more determined that I wouldn't be an accomplice. My time treating Joe had made me care about his well-being just as much as I would care about any other patient's, if not more so.

All the same, it seemed utterly hopeless to think that I could do anything without breaking the law. If I went to the authorities—the police or the medical board—I'd probably end up committed myself for claiming that a thirty-year-long history of mental illness was the product of such an elaborate conspiracy, and all on the word of a mental patient with a terrifying list of injured, suicidal, or dead patients and staff in his file. If I resigned in protest, it'd just leave Joe at the mercy of someone with fewer scruples than I. And I knew with absolute certainty that under no circumstances would I become a willing participant in this contemptibly inhuman treatment of a patient. I had gone into medicine to stop that sort of thing. I could, of course, go on treating Joe as I would a normal patient, try to be as kind to him as I suspected Nessie had been, and generally do my best to make his continued captivity as pleasant as possible. But even that kind of passive participation galled me. How many people had rationalized complicity in the cruel treatment of other "problem" patients, patients like my mother, thanks to the lure of a paycheck and an unwillingness to rock the boat?

The whole situation felt wrong, and my options had gone from bad to worse.

There was only one thing for it. I'd have to find a way to break him out in secret. If the attempt failed, I told myself, I had to hope the worst they would do is fire me. Sure, I could be banned from practicing medicine again if they pressed charges, but if Dr. G— was vindictive enough to try that, at least I could take a stab at trying to expose the whole thing before she got her way, seeing as I wouldn't have anything else to lose. And yes, I know what you are thinking, considering what had happened with Nessie. It *was* possible they could do worse, but surely I could find a way to protect myself?

And if I succeeded? Well, I would've let a somewhat paranoid but essentially stable patient out into society, and I could continue working at the hospital with a clean conscience, knowing the conspiracy was over.

Before I did anything, I consulted Jocelyn. If something went wrong, it would affect my whole life, which meant it would have an impact on hers. She quizzed me about how certain I was that Joe wasn't a danger. Then she asked if I trusted myself. I didn't quite know how to answer; the question had thrown me. So she said, "If you don't trust yourself, how can you expect anyone, whether it's your patients, colleagues, or even me, to trust you?"

So, there it was. Just a month after getting access to the patient who I was sure would make my career once I figured out his previously unknown condition, I was about to potentially wreck my career by letting him loose.

Not that breaking a patient out of any mental hospital, let alone this one, would be easy. Security cameras were fairly ubiquitous on the premises, and the staff kept a close eye on who had the key to any locked rooms or wards. If I wanted to do this and at least try to protect myself, it'd have to look like an accident.

My plan would have a chance only if the hospital were operating with a skeleton crew, so I opted to work late in the weeks before making my attempt. This would give me a sense of who was around during the hospital's off-hours, and, more importantly, no one would think anything of seeing me in the hospital at those times. And because I'd agreed to take on so much extra work after Nessie died, I actually needed time in the hospital.

As to the plan itself, it involved leaving my lab coat (and keys) in Joe's room, supposedly by accident, then setting off an equally accidental fire alarm, which would cause most of the staff to evacuate the hospital, clearing the way for Joe's escape. I also made sure Joe knew the way out by putting a floor plan of the hospital, with all the less used fire exits marked, inside a pack of gum which I then gave to him.

In retrospect, it was a terribly easy plan to botch, and Joe himself called me out on that when I told him about it.

"Doc, you're crazier than I am," he said with his characteristic crooked smile. "If that plan works, I'm Mickey Mouse."

"It will work," I told him. "The staff are lazy, you don't have a history of trying to break out, and no one will expect anyone to help you escape. Not after what happened with Nessie."

He shook his head fatalistically, but there was a gleam in his eye that told me I might have given him the first ounce of hope he'd had since being committed.

"Well, I won't start planning any trips, just in case," he said wryly. "But if they catch me and throw me back in here, I won't tell them it was your idea. Oh, and doc? God love ya for trying. If this works, I won't forget that I owe you a life's worth of freedom."

And that was it. All that was left was to carry out the plan. There I was, three weeks later, mildly nauseated from anxiety, my palms sweating, as I walked down the hallway towards Joe's room. The faint muttering and gibbering from the patients I knew to be insane were almost a demented mirror of my own scattered thoughts.

If I was caught, or he was, *would* they only fire me?

Or would they want to make an example of me to anyone else who knew the secret, or who pried too deeply into Joe's history?

Perhaps Nessie's death hadn't been clear enough.

Perhaps they really needed to send a message to anyone else who might have second thoughts.

I'd met Dr. G—, after all, and she hadn't seemed the type who might leave a loose end lying around.

I didn't really have to do this, did I?

I could just turn around and walk out now.

I *should* just turn around and walk out now. I had a fiancée. A life ahead of me. This wasn't any of my business. I didn't have to do this, did I?

But no, I knew I had to. It was the right thing to do, and I was not going to make myself an accessory to what amounted to kidnapping and murder just because I was too afraid for my own skin. Besides, there was barely anyone on staff, and by the time my fire alarm had gone off, there'd be almost no one around to stop Joe from leaving. My plan was close to foolproof. It would be fine.

As I reached the door to Joe's room, the sound of heavy footsteps caught my ear, and I turned to see Hank, the orderly, walking slowly down the hallway with an armful of bedsheets.

Shit. What if he knew what I was doing? No, that was impossible. There was no way anyone would know. I just needed to stay in Joe's room until Hank moved on past this hallway. I could probably hear his footsteps even through Joe's door. It would be fine. It would all be fine.

I focused on keeping my breathing calm. It wouldn't help if I looked anxious. Then I turned the key to Joe's room, stepped inside, shut the door gingerly behind me, and turned to face him. He was standing with his back to me, looking out the window, and I barely paid much attention to him as I frantically pulled off my lab coat and laid it on his bed, then sat down and listened to Hank's footfalls.

"Doc?"

I turned to see Joe looking at me. There was a hungry, longing look in his eye, as of a starving man who knows he's about to have a feast and can't wait.

I raised my eyebrows at him. "Yeah, Joe?"

"Thanks," Joe said, his voice a husky whisper. "This is exactly what I need."

His phrasing was a bit odd, but I didn't think much of it. I smiled at him.

"You're welcome."

And with that, I opened the door and stepped out into the hallway. I was about to turn and shut it again, when suddenly, a pair of hands as big as baseball mitts clamped themselves around my shoulders.

"Aren't you forgetting something, Parker?" boomed Hank's basso voice from just beside the door. I froze, my mind racing. The orderly chuckled in my ear. "For such a smart kid, you sure do stupid shit."

Then from behind me came the gravelly voice of Dr. P——. "Evening, *wonder boy.*"

Oh, *fuck me.*

"Well, I'll be. Speechless for once." Dr. P—— strolled around Hank, exultant, his face split into a ghoulish grin. He leaned in close enough that I could smell whiskey on his breath.

"Now, I'm gonna send someone to get your lab coat out of that room, but you and me? We're going to go talk to Dr. G—, and you're gonna tell her all about what you were planning to do with your newest patient in there tonight."

At those words, I began to struggle against Hank's grip, though it was like pulling at iron bars. "Let me go!" I kept my voice low. "I don't know what they've told you, but you don't understand, Hank. They're keeping a sane man in there! And he brings in so much money to this hospital that no one cares if he's sane! She might've killed Nessie to keep it secret, Hank. Let me go and talk to him, and you'll see. I swear, you'll see."

Dr. P— snickered. Hank didn't join in, but his grip didn't slacken. "Yeah, she said you'd say something like that. Sorry, kid. No can do."

The sheer crushing weight of my failure hit me all at once, and I was already jittery from the anxiety of doing something I knew was illicit. I was trying to suppress a groan of frustration when I heard something that spooked me.

Inside Joe's room, someone was laughing. But it wasn't Joe; it couldn't have been. It didn't sound human at all. Instead, what emerged from that room was a sepulchral, moist, hacking chuckle that sounded like it came from a rotting throat. It was a voice I'd heard before, the same laugh that had risen from the fetid pool of blood and piss in my dream as it dragged my mother into its depths.

A shiver knocked through me, but neither Hank nor Dr. P— reacted. It wasn't clear if they'd even heard it, and I didn't have the presence of mind to ask. All I could do was stare at Joe's door as Hank started to pull me away, that hoarse sound of nightmare echoing in the hallway and in my brain.

April 10, 2008

This part of the story is where things start to get really hard, and, honestly, it'd be a lot easier to just stop here. But in some sense, writing this is like sucking poison out of my system, albeit years after the fact. But I won't bore you with my agonizing.

Dr. P— gloated the entire way to the top floor and the medical director's office. "I had your number from the minute they hired you. When I heard they were bringing in some Ivy League wiseass to work on my staff, I knew you'd cause trouble. I told her everything was going fine, she shouldn't muck it up with some smarter-than-thou baby doc. But no, she was taking you on as a favor to an old friend. And to think, you were actually doing pretty well with your other patients, all things considered. Man, you high-and-mighty brats always think the sun shines out of each other's asses, so she even hoped you might actually get something out of Joe. But now she's gonna be *so disappointed.* I warned you, motherfucker. Don't forget that. You'd still be the golden boy if you'd listened to me. But you had to meddle with something you don't goddamn understand. You arrogant lightweight. You . . ."

Seriously, the jabber went on for the entire ten minutes it took to get to Dr. G—'s office.

I had no idea what was going to happen to me, and I was stumped as to what had gone wrong. I suppose I also felt a sort of relief at being caught, considering that lying and subterfuge were not my professional goals, but I was in agony that Joe remained trapped. At the same time . . . what the hell had I heard from Joe's room? I kept replaying the things Joe had said, then going back over Dr. G—'s warnings about his madness being contagious, wondering what was true. Or had everyone just been lying to me the whole time?

I'd felt that unholy laugh in my bones. Had my fears of being caught made me snap? Or, if I was sane, how had Joe mirrored a laugh pulled from my worst childhood nightmare?

My frantic, confused thoughts were interrupted as Hank yanked the door to Dr. G—'s office open and shoved me inside without a word. My nose nearly made contact with the carpet as I fell forward, and it took me a moment to steady myself and focus on the people in the room.

Yes, people. Dr. G— was there, of course, standing in front of her desk and glaring down at me with an expression that made me think of a hawk regarding a rotting carcass and deciding it wasn't worth eating. But seated behind her, in the well-crafted leather armchair usually reserved for the medical director, sat a wizened, tired old man in a heavily patched sport coat, regarding me with hard eyes over a pair of well-worn silver spectacles. I had no idea who this stranger was, but if Dr. G— was letting him use her chair, then he was obviously someone important. He looked far too old to be a plainclothes detective, as his wrinkled face and thinning silver hair marked him as a man who couldn't have been less than seventy or eighty years old. But who else could he be?

Dr. G— turned to Hank and Dr. P—, who'd mercifully closed his trap, though he still looked jubilant, and said, "Thank you, gentlemen. I'll take it from here." Then she came over and gently closed the door behind them as they departed.

The older man in the room with us cleared his throat and spoke with a patrician-sounding Mid-Atlantic accent that seemed oddly familiar, even though I couldn't place it.

"So this is the latest one, is it, Rose?"

Dr. G— didn't reply but simply nodded. The gesture immediately struck me as out of place, and in a moment, I realized why. Her expression as she'd inclined her head had none of the curtness or haughtiness she'd displayed toward me. Instead, it was soft in its deference. Not caring about the cause, but simply glad to have scented weakness, I pushed myself to my feet and jabbed my finger at her accusingly.

"Alright, I don't know if you're planning to fire me, or do something worse, but before you do, I want some *fucking*—"

"Parker—" began Dr. G—, but I barreled right over her.

"Answers! Did you think you could mislead me about a patient and that I'd take it lying down? Is all that crap in Joe's file just there to keep him here?"

"Parker—"

"And even if it isn't, why did you send your two thugs to spy on me every chance they got if you've got nothing to hide? Why'd you have one of them drag me here like I'm a prisoner? And how much have you been spying on me, if you knew what I was—"

"*PARKER.*"

Dr. G—'s white-hot voice seared the room, and almost by instinct, I shut up. The old man behind the desk chuckled.

"He's a feisty one. Reminds me of someone, Rose," he said. Dr. G—'s pained expression gave me another momentary bit of courage.

"And that's another thing. Who the hell are—"

"Parker, you are going to want to shut up and sit down right now before you say something we both regret." Dr. G— was barely taller than me in her heels, but her brutal aspect and ramrod-straight posture made her seem to tower over me. Not wanting to push any luck I might have, I cast my eyes around for the nearest chair and sat down immediately. She exhaled slowly and leaned back against her desk.

"Now," she said, "let's get one thing straight before we go any further, Parker. I have no intention of hurting you. And although you pushed your luck on this point *very* far, I am not going to fire you either."

My mouth fell open. She laughed.

"Quiet, I see. Good. Keep it that way, because as of now, you haven't said anything that suggests you've done anything wrong, and therefore, whatever you *might* have been planning to do in Joe's room tonight, we can both ignore it."

She gave me a pointed look before continuing. "Now, to answer both your implicit *and* explicit questions, I sent my orderlies to watch you because that has been standard procedure for every doctor Joe's had since 1973. Normally, we send them to watch only every few weeks, but the reaction you had after your first session with him convinced me we should keep you under more constant surveillance."

I started to ask a question, but her hand shot up so quickly that I clapped my mouth shut.

"First off, you spent almost twice as long in Joe's room as anyone else has on their first session. Secondly, you didn't look afraid so much as queasy and uncertain, neither of which portended that you'd gotten the same experience as his other doctors. In fact, the more we watched you, the less like his other doctors you became. For one thing, you kept going back in for similarly long sessions, and sometimes you even looked happy or relieved when you walked out. It didn't make any sense to the orderlies or to me. So I did what any physician faced with a mystery does. I got a second opinion."

"That's where I come in," said the older man.

"I'll get to you." Dr. G— shot a reproachful look over her shoulder at the old guy. She turned back to me.

"I suppose this is as good a time as any to introduce the two of you. Parker, meet Dr. Thomas A—, the first man to treat Joe and my earliest mentor as a psychiatrist."

Suddenly, I realized why I recognized his voice. It was an aged, slightly raspier version of the voice I'd heard on the tape of Joe's first session. I almost had trouble believing it. If Dr. A— was still alive, he must've been quite old. Still, he seemed lucid, even sharp. Right down to his eyes.

After surveying me for a moment, the older man nodded. "A pleasure, Parker. Though I really can't say I'm as impressed with you as I'd like to be. You might have the distinction of being the worst failure as a physician that Joe has ever had, given what we seem to have caught you trying to do."

The words were acid poured over an open wound. And it was a harshness delivered with such impersonal coolness. My face must have fallen, because the old man gave me an even sterner look.

"Not used to being told you're a fool, I see," he said. "Well, you are, and thank God you're a predictable one. Otherwise your idiocy might have done real damage. And now, you want to know how we knew. Rose told me that your greatest fear is not being able to save someone you care about. She also told me that there was no one on staff after Nessie who mattered to you, and that everyone who did matter was likely well out of reach of anyone locked in this hospital. It followed from those facts that Joe would torture you by making you care about *him*, and then fail to save him."

He turned to Dr. G——. "I don't blame you for not seeing it, Rose. You fell victim to a similar bit of trickery, if I recall correctly."

Dr. G—— flushed, which made Dr. A—— roll his eyes. "Yes, I know, you hate having your foolishness pointed out just as much as our boy here, but you were young. You grew out of it."

He turned back to me. "Which is something you'll have to do, and fast, after that stunt you pulled tonight, Parker. Like Bruce P—, I'd have fired you. That man's an oaf, but he knows how to protect this institution. Fortunately for you, Rose has a high opinion of your intellect and thinks you might be able to give us some insight into that walking mental plague we call a patient."

"That's enough, Thomas," said Dr. G—. "I don't want to make the poor kid quit just yet, and you're showing off. Plus there's more to this lesson.

"Parker, I keep referring to what you were planning to do in the vaguest possible terms for the sake of plausible deniability. We have only one person who claims to have heard you confess your intentions, and given who that is, we can dismiss it so long as you don't say anything explicitly confessional. Now, I'm going to tell you who our witness is, but before I do, you havc to promise that you're not going to say something stupid that confirms the accusation. Deal?"

I was utterly bewildered, but I nodded slowly. At that point, I was still coming down from the relief and gratitude I felt toward her for making such an effort to help me retain my position.

"Good. Parker, we brought you here because one of Joe's orderlies reported to us that he had been told you were planning to help Joe escape from the hospital. The person who told him was Joe himself."

Even if I'd wanted to confess, I couldn't have. I was struck dumb by this news; my spine was ice; my mouth was dry; and, I felt like I might throw up if I tried to speak. Seeing my expression, Dr. G— opened a drawer in her desk and pulled out a bottle of Scotch and a crystal rocks glass. She poured a generous amount into the glass and handed it to me.

"You look like you need it. Doctor's orders."

Despite the roiling in my stomach, I did as she directed. At first, it made me feel sicker, but then a numbing warmth spread over my brain and I felt my muscles relax ever so slightly. It was a welcome relief after what I'd just heard. Dr. G— gave me a sympathetic look. Dr. A—, however, only looked grim.

"Rose, this miscreant doesn't need to be comforted. He needs to be debriefed. He might have spent more time actually talking to Joe than most of the others. He needs to tell us what happened with Joe during their sessions."

Maybe it was the shock of what I'd just heard, maybe it was all my anger looking for a new outlet after everything that had motivated it had been stripped away, or maybe it was the Scotch, but something snapped in me. I was sick of being talked about so dismissively, a naughty child who wasn't even in the room. I was sick of these revelations being dumped on me without getting a chance to process them. But some things had clicked into place, and more than anything else, I was sick to my stomach at the thought that I might have been set up to fail.

I glared at Dr. A—, filling my gaze with enough contempt to match his cool, disdainful look a hundred times over. "Not a chance, old man. From what I've gathered, you and your 'student' here put me on a collision course with someone you fully expected to hurt me and didn't tell me everything you knew before I went in. I wasn't supposed to cure him, was I? I was just a lab rat for you and her, because you wanted to see what he did to me. Well, I'm done with it. If you want to know what I found out from talking to him, then you have to let me in on what you know. All of it. Like why she tried to commit suicide, or why you gave up on treating him in the first fucking place, or why you kept putting vulnerable patients in harm's way long after you knew what he was capable of."

Dr. A— appeared unruffled, though I could tell that whatever air of geniality he'd tried to assume had dropped as soon as I'd finished speaking. The effect would've cowed me if I hadn't been so full of my own righteous anger. I'd felt like a small animal staring down a predator when facing Dr. G—, but meeting the bloodless, icy gaze of that hunched old man, I barely felt acknowledged as a living being. More like a statistic that had the effrontery to talk back. But I didn't back down. I met his eyes for a long, terrible moment before he finally settled back in his chair and expelled an irritated snort.

"Well, there's probably no harm in giving you a bit more information," he said. "Lord knows I have little enough to do tonight. But understand this, Parker. If you want to hear all the details, then you'll start by accepting this: There is no curing that horror downstairs. There is only containing him."

"I'm his doctor," I said. "I'll be the judge of that."

"Yes, I suppose you will," he said softly. "But just as you were earlier this evening, you are wrong on a very important point: *You* are not his doctor. You are, and have only *ever* been, just a tool to get data on him. *I* am his doctor, and I have borne that cross since he first entered this hospital. It took away my career, and it's going to take away my retirement. It is my life's work. It would have been Rose's when I'm gone, but I don't intend to leave it unsolved that long. You do not and will *never* understand what it is to be the last person standing between Joe and a world that cannot understand or resist him. So keep a civil tongue in your head from now on or you'll find yourself on the curb."

Anger tempted me to reply, but some part of me knew it would be a terrible idea. This was all the concession I was going to get out of this bitter, proud man, and it was more than I had any right to expect. So, forcing my frustration down to a simmer, I gave him the most deferential nod I could manage. It seemed to appease him.

"Well, then," he said. "Rose, why don't you tell him about the last smart, headstrong young doctor to try and treat our pet monster?"

I looked up at Dr. G—, and to my surprise, she wasn't looking at me with the aloof air she'd worn before. Instead, her eyes were filled with sadness and pity.

"I'm so sorry," she mouthed, so that only I could see. Then she began speaking in the crisp voice of a scientist presenting her findings.

"When I began to treat Joe, he was only six years old and had been admitted to the hospital barely a month before he was assigned to me. At the time, as you know from reading my notes, my theory was simple: that he was showing the signs of sadistic personality disorder and sociopathy as a result of post-traumatic stress disorder brought on by his years of untreated night terrors, which were so successful at disturbing him because of his apparently comorbid sleep paralysis and acute entomophobia. His evident psychological progeria was simply a defense mechanism designed to make him seem as if he had more control over the situation than he did, and his monstrous behavior was an act designed to make him feel more confident in facing the monster he imagined. Frankly, I thought the whole thing was embarrassingly easy and a waste of my time, as you probably guessed from my notes."

She paused to collect her thoughts, then continued speaking. "My proposed course of treatment was to get him to face the trauma of his night terrors through a combination of hypnosis therapy, talk therapy, and the use of sedatives when he slept in order to prevent the nightmares from manifesting. This much you also know from the notes. However, what you may not know is that my treatment worked. Spectacularly. Joe barely showed any signs of the disorders I'd heard reported in Dr. A—'s initial diagnosis after the first couple of days. Rather, something else manifested. He became very . . . attached to me."

She swallowed, and I could tell the memories were still painful. "It's not an exaggeration to say that Joe began relating to me as if I were a surrogate mother. I'd already guessed that his parents were distant, given their conspicuous absence from the hospital, so this was not much of a surprise. Still, the more attached he got, the more he seemed to heal, and the more and more devoted he became. He seemed less and less like a proto-sociopath and more and more like a frightened young child."

Her voice faltered. "You have to understand something before I go any further. I'd also had a very chilly relationship with my parents from early on and had almost no friends even through my medical school days. I rarely dated, and I've never married or had children because I simply don't let people get close to me if I can help it. However . . . something in the way Joe related to me brought out all my mothering instincts. For the first time in my life, I felt needed and loved unconditionally, and while I tried to keep my professional distance, there was just something about him that made my defenses against affection melt. And the more nurturing I became, the more his condition seemed to improve."

The tears in her eyes were obvious now, and she blinked them back hastily, even as her voice became brittle with the strain. "I was sure I'd be able to get him discharged around my fourth month, and so, as a final experiment to test his ability to empathize, I let him have a pet. A little cat, because I'd grown up with cats, and I thought he might relate to them the same way I had, being someone who had trouble around other people. I don't recall what he called her. Something about a flower, I think."

"Fiberwood Flower," I said softly.

She looked at me, wide-eyed. "Yes. Yes, exactly. How did you—"

"Just finish the story, Rose," said Dr. A——. "We'll be able to find out what he knows much quicker once you've finished."

Dr. G—— sucked in her breath and nodded, her sharp veneer covering her previous vulnerability like a well-worn mask. "Anyway. I gave him Fiberwood Flower and made Dr. A—— agree that if he took care of her properly for a week, that would prove he'd been cured of his antisocial tendencies."

Her face clouded, but not with sadness this time. With anger. "He treated that poor cat like an angel for six days, and then on the last day, when I walked into his room, I found her corpse lying on the ground with her head ripped off. And just above her corpse, he'd scrawled an arrow pointing down in her blood, with the inscription 'for Nosey Rosie.'"

Her voice had become as hard as diamonds. "Now, no one's called me 'Nosey Rosie' since I got teased on the playground at his age, and I don't think he ever heard anyone call me by my first name. He shouldn't have even begun to be able to guess at that name. But he had. And as soon as I walked in, he started laughing. And—and I'd still swear to this years after it happened—it sounded *exactly* like the laughter of this one child in particular who used to bully me when I was his age. Between that voice and the bloody mess that had been an adorable cat that this *child* had mutilated . . . I snapped. I ran out of that room, submitted my resignation, and . . . well, you know the rest."

Her expression seethed with fury and hurt. I reached an arm up to her out of reflexive empathy, but she swatted it away before I could get very far, with an expression that said no matter how much it hurt to remember this, she still had her pride and wasn't going to suffer the pity of a subordinate. I settled for trying to give her a look that was both sympathetic and respectful.

Then I heard Dr. A——'s voice from behind her. "So, Parker, you still think you can cure the little bastard? Care to suggest a diagnosis for someone who was able to just instantly pull an old schoolyard taunt out of thin air to mock a woman whose vulnerable spots he'd been able to reach as if by magic? Well?"

Hating myself for it, I shook my head helplessly. "I didn't know. I didn't . . . I . . . I don't know."

"Of course you don't." There was a note of satisfaction in the old man's voice. "You have no idea what's wrong with him. What's more, you've bought into all the mythology surrounding him because you're young, you're impressionable, and you don't know any better. That's why you're not his doctor. I am his doctor. And I do know better."

April 20, 2008

Hey, guys, sorry to have taken a little longer to update, but I really did have to make sure I got my memory of this particular series of events as exact as possible, because otherwise my actions from this point onward wouldn't make any sense. I hope I succeeded.

As he finished his last words, Dr. A— gripped the legs of his chair and stood up slowly and gingerly, as if every bone in his body might snap if he moved too fast. Despite his age, I could tell that he'd once cut an imposing figure. Even with his slight stoop, he looked to be at least six feet two, and he probably would've been at least an inch taller if he'd stood up straight. He grabbed one edge of the desk to steady himself and held out the other hand to Dr. G—, who reached down and picked up an ornate cane made of dark wood with a bronze head in the shape of a falcon. He took it from her and slowly made his way around the desk to me. As he did so, I saw that he was clutching a thick, dusty file, which surely must have been copied from the very documents I'd seen.

He sat down on the desk and gave me another flinty look.

"Before I go on, you have to understand something," he began. "If I am right about what is wrong with Joe, then we really are doing a service by keeping him here, not just to the outside world, but to Joe himself. If his parents were less endowed with financial and legal power, we would have done a lot more by now. However, we cannot afford the kind of legal battle that my suspicions would bring, if reported. So we are doing the only thing we can do and keeping him here. Got it?"

I nodded, this time with sincere deference. He smiled gruffly in acknowledgment. Then, with a grim flourish, he opened Joe's file to the first page.

"When I first met Joe"—he rapped the black-and-white photo of a wolfish child—"he seemed like a normal boy with a case of night terrors. But, of course, I got him wrong. Disastrously wrong. When he came back, he was violent and incapable of speech. I was flummoxed. I had no idea what I'd done wrong. What was more, I had no idea why his tactics kept changing. You must've noticed. He went from making people feel like dirt to making them too scared to stay in the same room. Well, when I resigned as medical director, I was still no closer to constructing an explanation than I was at the beginning. But retirement's given me nothing but time to check his old case notes, and the more I looked, the more it slowly started to make sense."

He turned a few pages and poked the file with his finger. "The first brainwave came when I worked out why his delusions kept changing. They shift every time someone calls him a new nasty name. Take when we brought him in. He wouldn't even speak. But then a nurse called him a 'bad boy,' and he suddenly started taunting people. You might not think that means all that much, but I've been to see the therapists who treated everyone who survived him during those first few years, and you know what they all told me? All of them, Rose included, said the same thing: he called them names that were directed at them when they were growing up, mostly by bullies or nasty other kids. None of it was too specific, but he seemed to know which playground taunts would work best for every single one of them. You see it now? Someone calls him a 'bad boy,' well, he throws taunts until he works out what the worst boy on earth would be for each of them and then acts like *that*."

More pages were turned. "Now look at this. After years berating people this way, he finally meets a violent patient who won't take his crap. But what does that patient do? He beats him half to death and calls him a 'fucking monster.' Next thing you know, he's acting like the monster that used to chase one of our orderlies in his dreams, and probably like the monsters that used to scare the crap out of his other roommates. That's why the first kid's heart stopped, why he started trying to rape a sexual assault victim, and why he could scare someone enough to get him to break the iron bars off his window. Because if he's going to be a monster, he's going to be the worst monster that each of his victims can imagine. Instead of making them feel as terrible as they felt at their worst moments of feeling like shit, now he's going to scare them as much as they've ever been scared in their lives."

He lowered his spectacles and regarded me for a moment before continuing. "Now, surely a bright resident like you will have realized that this kind of behavior tells us that whatever else might be wrong with him, we can conclude that Joe is extremely suggestible. At bare minimum, this implies something very unpleasant about his upbringing, because children his age aren't usually this willing to internalize negative feedback unless they've been conditioned by their parents. And we have strong evidence from my first session with him supporting the idea that Joe was horribly abused. Rose, if you would?"

Dr. G— pulled open another drawer and took out a cassette tape player and two tapes. I recognized them as copies of the ones I had. She inserted one in her desktop deck and hit Play. Dr. A—'s voice flowed out. I'd listened to the session before, but in the context of what I'd just heard, the words took on a grim significance.

> Dr. A—: Hello, Joe, my name is Dr. A—. Your parents tell me you have trouble sleeping. Could you tell me why that is?
>
> Joe: The thing in my walls won't let me.
>
> A: I see. I'm sorry to hear that. Could you tell me about the thing in your walls?
>
> J: It's gross.
>
> A: Gross? How so?
>
> J: Just gross. And scary.
>
> A: What I mean is, can you describe it?
>
> J: It's big and hairy. It's got fly eyes and two big, superstrong spider arms with really long fingers. Its body is a worm.

Dr. A— paused the tape. "Now, flies' eyes, along with being naturally alien-looking, don't blink. And the main characteristics he attributes to the creatures' arms are that they are big and strong, and presumably hairy, hence the reference to spiders. And its body is a worm. In other words, a phallus. So we have something phallic with big, strong, hairy arms and unblinking eyes. What could that be?"

He pushed play again. The voices restarted.

A: That does sound scary. And how big is it?

J: Big! Bigger than daddy's car!

The Pause button clicked again. "Now, why only call it 'daddy's car'?"

"I mean, his parents were rich enough to keep him here since the '70s," I said without thinking. "It's possible both parents had their own cars."

"Wrong," snapped Dr. A——. "I asked, and they had only one car, and they both used it. So why use that particular reference point for this monster's size? That's quite a specific free association, I'd say. Now, why would Joe free-associate his father after talking about something phallic with hairy arms that held him down and stared at him? Curiouser and curiouser. But let's not get ahead of ourselves. First, let's see how his parents react to this alleged intruder."

A: I see. And have your parents ever seen it?

J: No. It goes back in the walls when they come.

A: Something that big can fit in your walls? They don't break?

J: It melts. Like ice cream. It looks like it is the wall.

"So his parents don't acknowledge this thing's existence," said Dr. A——. "Now, why might that be? If you are following my train of thought, I would think the father's reason for not seeing a monster would be obvious. But the mother? Perhaps she simply refused to acknowledge what Joe's father was doing, even with him standing right there by the bed. Joe couldn't have processed that his mother was in denial, so the only logical conclusion would be that his father must've tricked his mother into thinking that he, the father, was part of the wall. It would fit. Now let's get to the real meat."

A: I see. And it's what made those marks on your arms?

J: Yes. I tried covering my face so I wouldn't have to see it. It pulled my arms away and made me open my eyes with its fingers.

A: Why did it do that?

J: It likes when I feel bad. That's why it doesn't let me sleep.

A: What do you mean?

J: It eats bad thoughts.

"The answer was there all the time." Dr. A— stared at the tape player in a kind of disconsolate fascination. "I just hadn't paid enough attention. Joe was telling us that he was being sexually abused. He described the sensation of being held down and raped by his father in the context of a monster that has all the same attributes of a grown man raping a small boy. He even gave us a clue that his father was a sadist by telling us that the monster ate bad thoughts, which would be what a sadist getting off on his own cruelty would seem to be doing to a young child. What's more, Joe's initial passiveness and subsequent extreme suggestibility when called nasty names are consistent with the behavior of an extremely abused child before and after a psychotic break."

He sighed. At this point, he was talking as much to himself as to me. "Of course, that leaves us with the puzzle of why Joe would mimic his father's own sadism when we brought him back in. Well, that brings us to the last part of the tape."

A: I see. Well, in that case, I think I know how we can get rid of it.

J: Really?!

A: Yes. If it eats bad thoughts, then I want you to have nothing but good thoughts when it comes.

J: How'm I supposed to do that? It's scary!

A: I think it wants you to think it's scary, Joe. But you know what? It's not. It's just your imagination. Do you know what an imagination is?

J: Sorta.

A: Then you know it's the part of you that comes up with ideas. Sometimes they're good, and sometimes they're scary. And ideas can seem dangerous. But Joe, even if your ideas seem scary, they're still *your* ideas. And your imagination can't scare you with them unless you let it.

J: So I can control it?

A: That's right, Joe.

J: How do you know?

A: That's my job, to know. My special power is to stop people being scared. Which is why people come here to not be scared anymore. And you know what, Joe? All of those people are only scared because of ideas. Because of parts of them that they can't control.

J: Wow.

A: Yes. Now, I'll bet you're a big boy who doesn't wet his bed anymore, aren't you, Joe?

J: Gross! Duh!

A: Well, think of that big, scary monster like wetting the bed. It's just a part of you that you allowed to get out of control.

J: That's funny. The monster is my peepee.

A: Not exactly. But they're both things you can control because they're part of you, Joe. Now, does that monster seem so scary anymore?

J: No! It's just me scaring myself. And I'm going to tell it that I know that the next time I see it!

Dr. A—— stopped the tape, and I could tell that those last moments had drained him.

"This is why I'll never let his case go." His voice was barely above a whisper. "Because I think, in my arrogance, I created the problems he has now. I think that between our first two sessions, because of what I told him, Joe went from believing he was the target of a monster that lives on people's psychoses to believing he *was* the monster. Think what that would do to a child who was the victim of sexual abuse. They're already at higher risk for dissociation. What I told Joe . . . it might have simply pushed him into full-blown dissociative identity disorder, because the thought that he was responsible for his own abuse would've been too much to bear. So he created a second 'monster' personality to blame it on that mimics the sadism he experienced from his father. And because we didn't see it, now . . . now that 'monster' personality is so completely in control of his psyche that his mind and behavior have begun adapting to fulfill its imagined needs. Even just believing he was *a* monster this completely would be bad enough, as it would make him probably the purest sadistic psychopath in the history of psychiatry. But this is worse. This *particular* monster truly believes that he needs to be constantly exposed to bad thoughts in order to survive, the same way you or I need food. As a result, his sense of empathy has evolved to be able to figure out how to trigger psychosis within seconds of meeting someone.

"And not only that, but because of his residual suggestibility, he can trigger different forms of misery on command. His delusions are so strong, in other words, that they've tricked his mind into being able to do things no human mind should be able to do. Now, granted, it may be that all the people who say he triggered their bad memories and worst fears are just sharing the same delusion, or might have forgotten that they revealed key details in his hearing. But even if that were true, one thing is undeniable: he's developed an ability to induce suicide in people as a defense mechanism, much the same way his original personality 'died' to make room for the monstrous one. And it's worked perfectly. Until now."

He flipped the file shut and looked at me again, his eyes boring into mine. "That is why we need you. You aren't dead and you experienced his tricks firsthand. You might be the only witness we have, aside from Rose, who treated him when he was far less advanced and did it so long ago that we can't be sure her account is still accurate. You're the only person who can provide us a fully accurate debriefing on how he went about manipulating you."

With that, he put one thin, but surprisingly strong hand under my chin and held my face in place as he spoke his next words.

"So I'll ask you one more time, Parker. Tell me, for Joe's sake, if not for mine, *what happened between him and you?*"

At that point, I had no reason to withhold anything anymore. So I told them. I told them about Joe's seeming sanity, his extremely tidy explanation of his own confinement, and his reappropriation of the Fiberwood Flower incident. I told them about his perfectly calculated story of feeling guilty for his mother's injuries, just as I had once felt guilty for my own mother's problems. I told them how deftly he exploited my grief over Nessie's death. I even told them how Dr. P——, with his warnings not to bother trying to cure anyone and his ham-fisted attempts at intimidation, had made it so easy to believe Joe. They listened attentively to the whole story, and when I'd finished, Dr. A— looked like he felt his age.

"So," he said, "he didn't rely on any details about your own life, then. He simply worked out that you were an empathetic person and played on that. It's likely a coincidence that he selected something about his mother that mirrors your own feelings of responsibility for your mom. Most boys are sensitive about their mothers. What's more, he blamed the mistreatment of his pet cat on his father, presumably because that's the personality that was responsible. So he was finally able to open up about his anger at his own abuse, even if indirectly. You actually might have solved his case, after all, Parker. Thank you. Rose, I think we've solved this particular puzzle. We obviously can't tell Joe's parents what we know, so just inform them that we've concluded that his case really is incurable, and he'll have to stay here indefinitely for his own good. As for Parker, take him off the case."

"No!" Something felt desperately wrong about Dr. A—'s explanation. The older man turned to me with an incredulous look.

"No?" he asked. "Parker, the case is solved. You just confirmed our hypothesis, and even if you hadn't, believe me, it would take a psychiatrist with far more experience than you to even begin to make that poor young man healthy. Even if I were still practicing—"

"But you're not. You retired. And I don't think you got it right. Something doesn't fit."

"How dare you?! You ju—"

"Relax, Thomas," said Dr. G——. "If Parker has another idea, I want to hear it. It can't hurt to get a second opinion."

Dr. A—— grumbled but waved his hand at me with evident irritation.

Starting to feel nervous again, I cleared my throat and began speaking before the tension could stop me.

"Before I try to advance my theory, I want to ask a few more questions just to make sure I've got some of the details right," I said.

"Oh, for the love of—," Dr. A—— began, but Dr. G—— put up her hand.

"Yes, Parker?"

"I want to start with the night terrors," I said. "Did Joe ever mention them after he came back in?"

Dr. A—— looked as if he was about to give a curt reply, but then a thoughtful look flashed across his face.

"Now that you mention it, no," he said. "Though by that point it might have been too late. Besides, he was sedated, and his father probably didn't enjoy it without him experiencing the pain."

"Maybe," I said, turning to Dr. G——. "But I'm not sure that explanation of the origins of his 'monster' is right. Dr. G—, didn't you say Joe was suffering from entomophobia?"

Dr. G— nodded slowly. She seemed unsure where I was going with this. "Yes, it was something his parents mentioned when they first brought him in."

"And was he afraid of bugs when you treated him?" I asked.

"Not particularly," she said. "We tried some exposure therapy, but he didn't react much like an entomophobe."

"Obviously the entomophobia was just a proxy for what he thought he was experiencing," said Dr. A—. "Rose, really—"

"Dr. A—," I said, "would you please play that description of the monster in Joe's wall again?"

Dr. A— gave me a long, tired look, but he complied and started skipping through the tape until he hit the relevant passage.

```
It's big and hairy. It's got fly eyes
and two big, superstrong spider arms
with really long fingers. Its body is a
worm.
```

"That *would* upset an entomophobe more than anything, don't you think?" I asked.

"Again, not surprising if the entomophobia was a result of what he thought was hurting him," scoffed Dr. A—.

"True," I said. "But there's something else. Can you skip to the part where you tell him it's his imagination?"

Sighing, Dr. A— ran the tape forward.

```
A: Well, think of that big, scary mon-
   ster like wetting the bed. It's just
   a part of you that you allowed to get
   out of control.

J: That's funny. The monster is my pee-
   pee.

A: Not exactly. But they're both things
   you can control because they're part
   of you, Joe. Now, does that monster
   seem so scary anymore?

J: No! And I'm going to tell it that it
   doesn't scare me the next time I see
   it!
```

The tape stopped. Dr. A— appeared increasingly annoyed, and Dr. G— still looked puzzled.

"He doesn't sound like a rape victim who's just been told it's his own fault, does he? He sounds relieved. He sounds happy. That's not what you expect from someone going through a dissociative episode. And if he was as suggestible as you say, why didn't he start acting like he was the monster right then? Why still retain his old self?"

"His mind probably hadn't fully processed it yet," Dr. A— murmured, barely paying attention.

"Or," I said, "there was no dissociative episode. In fact, what if there was no parental abuse, or even no night terrors? What if Joe really was being tortured by something that knew how to play to his entomophobia and knows how to play just as skillfully to everyone else's fears? And what if, when he told it that it was part of him, it *became* the second personality that you think is the result of abuse? What if he brought the monster in here with him when he came back?"

"Oh yes, and I'm sure his head spins on its axis and he spits pea soup," scoffed Dr. A—, starting to sound legitimately angry. "Stop talking like an overenthusiastic horror fan, son, and get ahold of yourself. You're a scientist, for God's sake."

"Just hear me out," I said. "I wouldn't have believed it myself before tonight, but the thing is . . ."

I found myself breathing uneasily. "Look, I know you want to dismiss all that knowledge he has as some kind of fluke or think that people don't remember what they've told him, but I know that's not true in my case. When Hank was dragging me away from his room, he started laughing in exactly the same voice as something I still have nightmares about. And I guarantee you, after the warning Dr. G— gave me, I never told him anything about my issues or what frightened me. So how did he know the exact right tone and timbre to use?"

"You heard what you wanted to hear," Dr. A— snapped. "You expected a monster's voice. Your mind reacted by pretending it was hearing the right one."

"But that's just it—I didn't. Remember, I thought he was a sane, mistreated patient when Hank grabbed me, yet I *still* heard that voice. Just when I would *least* expect something supernatural, it happened anyway. And what if the others, like Dr. G—, aren't lying? What if they really did never tell him anything, and yet he still knew how to scare them?"

"He has a point, Thomas. I'll grant you that I don't have the notes to prove it, but I have no idea how Joe would've found out about people calling me 'Nosey Rosie.' I can't remember the topic ever coming up anywhere that he possibly could've overheard it. I don't think I even remembered that nickname until I found it scrawled on the wall of his room."

"He might've heard your name from someone and guessed it by luck, Rose!" Dr. A— exploded. "Not many derogatory words rhyme with your name. It's not hard for a child to work out!"

"You should know better than to dismiss symptoms as coincidence in order to save your theory, Thomas," Dr. G— said softly.

Dr. A— looked furious. "All right." Venomous sarcasm poured through his voice. "Suppose you're both right, even though it breaks our entire commitment to science into little pieces. What treatment can you suggest for treating a case of possession by the bogeyman, then? Do we pump his stomach? Drill a hole in his skull to let the demon out? Enlighten me."

"You said you'd ruled out other possibilities," I continued. "I don't suppose you had someone perform an exorcism?"

"What sort of quack do you think I—"

"Oh, stop trying to pretend you're the purest scientist in the room, Thomas," Dr. G— snapped. "Sure, you kept it off the books, but we both know you tried a couple of unconventional things with Joe."

Dr. A— didn't answer her, but for the first time, he looked visibly uncomfortable.

"If you don't tell him, Thomas, I will."

"Oh, for heaven's sake, Rose, we ruled that nonsense out, and you know it. Why encourage this overly imaginative, insubordinate pup you've hired with useless data?"

"So you did try an exorcism," I said coolly. "What happened?"

"What happened was exactly what you'd expect from a troublemaker like Joe," snarled Dr. A—. "The priest came in, started saying his rites, and it didn't do a damn thing. All Joe did was fuck with him the entire time, saying he was an angel sent to earth from the right hand of Christ and that the priest was betraying his own God. Exactly the sort of thing anyone would say to discombobulate a religious person."

"And I'll bet it *really* discombobulated that *particular* priest, didn't it?" I pressed. "I'll bet he couldn't even finish the ritual, could he?"

"He . . . he left early, yes," said Dr. A——. "What's your point?"

"And did you try and record the process?"

"Of course not!" Dr. A—— sputtered. "I don't want anyone *knowing* I entertained that kind of crankery!"

"Pity," I said. "Because I'll bet you anything that if you had recorded it, you wouldn't have picked him up saying anything. Because the patient you have in there—Joe himself—he's not the one doing this. Whatever came with Joe is what's doing this, and it's using him as a scapegoat."

"You seriously think some bogeyman is living rent-free in our hospital?" Dr. A—— asked, disdainful laughter twisting beneath the surface of his voice. "Rose, you might want to call Hank back with a straitjacket. I think our would-be savior here has gone insane himself."

"There may be a way for me to see if I'm right," I said, focusing on the more amenable Dr. G——. "I know it's a strange hypothesis, but if you let me gather enough data to test it and it turns out wrong, you can take me off the case."

Dr. G—— tapped the fingers of both hands together and considered me for a few seconds. She looked intrigued in spite of herself. Finally, she waved her hand. "Go on."

I took a breath. "With your permission. I'd like to have tomorrow off so I can go talk to the only people who *can* confirm or deny both of these hypotheses, even indirectly. I'd like to visit Joe's family and have a look at the room where this happened."

"Oh yes, that will go wonderfully," sneered Dr. A—. "What are you planning to say? 'Excuse me, Mr. M—, but did you get off on molesting your child and hearing his screams? Did the property happen to come with a warning that it might have a giant bug infestation?'"

"We both know there are subtler ways than that to look for clues that people are sadistic," I said, trying to avoid taking the bait. "And anyway, I'm only trying to see if my hypothesis has any sort of leg to stand on, and that won't set off their alarm bells at all. They'll feel completely comfortable, so if Joe's parents are closet sadists, the clues should be fairly easy to spot. And if there's any evidence that something supernatural lived in his walls, or that the house was haunted in any way, that should be easy to find, too."

I stared squarely into Dr. A—'s eyes. "And you know what? Even if I don't see any evidence that the parents are off, if there's no evidence of anything supernatural there either, then I'll admit you were right and that my brain got caught up in antiscientific nonsense. Good enough?"

Once more, we looked at each other for a long moment, and by the time the gaze was broken, I could tell that he had made his peace with the idea, even if he couldn't bring himself to respect me for entertaining it. Then my eye caught movement, and I turned to see that Dr. G— had pulled out a pen and scribbled down a note in her calendar.

She looked up at me. "Yes, you can have the day off. Regardless of what Thomas says, I want to know what you find. Don't worry, I'll tell Bruce that you're on an assignment at my request. I don't believe the family ever moved, so use the address in his file. Now go home and get some sleep if you can. We need you alert tomorrow."

April 24, 2008

I underestimated how hard it would get to write this story the deeper I got into it. Believe me, I wish I could have had this particular part of the story posted sooner, but as I think you'll see, the subject matter made that impossible. I swear I'm not trying to milk this or draw it out unnecessarily. It just is that hard to remember and recount, to get my head back in this space. That said, when I do sit down to lay it out, the story pours out. Sort of like an infected sore that's just been lanced. I do feel loads better with each installment.

If you've been with me this long, thank you for your patience. If you're looking for an answer to the mystery of this story, this is probably the post you've been waiting for.

I wish I could say I followed Dr. G——'s instructions and slept like a baby when I got home that night, but the fact is that what I'd learned made sleep virtually impossible. My brain was on a hamster wheel, wondering at my own increasing willingness to entertain erratic, absurd theories. Just a week ago, I was convinced that Joe was a sane man trapped by a group of criminal medical professionals. I got caught trying to set him *free*. Now I was going on a field trip to see if I could find proof that he'd been possessed by . . . what, exactly? A demon? A vengeful spirit? The bogeyman? Don't all crazy people think they're the rational ones? And who was to say I hadn't just snapped the way all of Joe's other doctors had, and that Dr. G——'s staff would be waiting with a straitjacket when I finally went back to the hospital? Come to think of it, I wouldn't have blamed them if that had happened.

And thumping under everything alongside my heartbeat was the sound of that laughter from Joe's room.

Unfortunately, Jocelyn wasn't there to help me process any of this or, alternatively, take my mind off it. There was a note in the kitchen that she was having a late night at the library to make headway on the next segment of her writing. I texted to let her know I was home, and she called, eager to hear if I still had my job or if the police were arriving soon. I didn't want to get into it over the phone, so I reassured her that everything was fine, and I'd share the whole story when I saw her.

Eventually, desperate for sleep, I washed down a few antianxiety pills with a copious amount of wine, and somehow, the combination of chemicals finally made me fall asleep. However, the sound of my alarm, which rang seemingly the second after I'd closed my eyes, only compounded the horrors of the previous night with a splitting headache.

Still, a shower, ibuprofen, and a small ocean of coffee later, I felt functional enough to drive. So it was that I dug out my copy of Joe's file and looked at the first page to find his family's home address.

The location listed instantly explained how Joe's family could afford more than twenty-five years of inpatient treatment. It was located in a part of the state so infamous for its wealth that its very name conjured images of gold-plated cars, palatial homes, and family-owned yachts. What was more, a quick look at MapQuest showed that Joe's family home stood at the center of a vast estate bordering the water. Under any other circumstances, I'd have been at least a bit curious about what such opulence looked like up close, but in this case, the only thing that struck me was how isolated the place was, and therefore how far from help anyone there—particularly a small child—must've been. The one mercy was that it was only about an hour-and-a-half drive from New Haven and would be shorter if traffic was light. So, laying the MapQuest directions on the passenger seat of my car for easy reference, I began the drive out to find whatever might be waiting for me at the birthplace of Joe's insanity, if that was, indeed, what it was.

If I believed that nature had a sense of irony, that drive would have been a strong bit of evidence. The weather was the sort of cool autumn balm that one hopes and prays for every year, the traffic nonexistent, and, to top it off, I got a text from Jocelyn wishing me well and letting me know she'd be home in the evening, so we could catch up. In short, under any other circumstances, it would have been the perfect day, which made the drive into a secular equivalent of the mouth of Hell that much more unnerving.

The postcard picturesqueness of the part of the state where Joe's family lived only enhanced this cognitive dissonance. I must have driven past hundreds of expansive yet tasteful manses of the sort only old money could construct, each of which looked as if it belonged in a Jane Austen novel rather than in the United States. The few residents I saw out on the streets seemed to have been plucked from a Brooks Brothers or J. Press magazine spread, each decked out in clothes worth several months of my salary and watches that probably would've cost my annual income at least. My relatively modest, though well-kept Ford Taurus must have been conspicuously out of place alongside the armies of Mercedes, Audis, and Bentleys. I was surprised that anyone from a town like this would end up in a hospital at all, let alone at the Connecticut State Asylum. This was the sort of place where pain of any kind was either flushed out with medication and trips to boutique psychiatrists or kept at a respectable distance with copious expenditures. It was, in short, a place where anything unpleasant, let alone a supernatural horror, had been ruthlessly gentrified out of sight and out of mind.

It wasn't until I was pulling up to the heavy, wrought iron gate set into a high, thick, cobblestone wall at Joe's family estate that I felt any sense of ominousness in my surroundings. Though that may have partially been the result of being roared at by a burly security guard who looked like he should've been on a mission sponsored by Blackwater rather than guarding a quiet family home. Not wanting to seem unduly nervous, I explained in my best bedside manner that I was a doctor and had come to speak to the residents about their son.

He spun around with military precision and marched to his kiosk, where he dialed in a few numbers on his console. A woman's voice, tinged with the sort of polite, clenched-jaw accent that one usually heard only from elderly yacht club members, emerged from a microphone, and after a brief conversation with the martinet who'd just blockaded me, she agreed that I should be let in. The guard ended the communication smartly and pushed a button, causing the gate to swing open with almost perfect silence and smoothness. My stomach churning with the nerves I'd been trying to suppress since setting out this morning, I continued on my way.

The driveway to Joe's family home ran up a gradual, obsessively manicured hill surrounded by a small forest of equally well-kept sugar maples and northern red oak. At the top of the hill, encircled by beeches, stood the house itself—a towering, Gothic Revival stone manor that seemed to transform the sun's rays into a radiant pastel glow. I pulled up in front and, handing my keys to a stiff-necked valet who looked pained to even set foot in a car as modest as mine, stepped out to face whatever the house had in store for me.

However, the longer I stared at it, the more uneasy I felt. Frankly, if Joe's family had lived in a castle built of pitch-black stone covered in screaming demonic gargoyles and permanently backlit by lightning flashes, I think I would have found it less unsettling. The place was colossal: so large that it could have housed an entire school and still looked spacious. I'm pretty sure it rivaled CSA's main building in size. Its ornamentation was superfluously pleasant, with plenty of stone roses and cupids smiling from its many windowsills and ramparts, not to mention the numerous hand-carved lattices and copious amounts of stained glass. But even to my untrained eye, this finery looked like a tacked-on, glittering mask for what was essentially a spartan, forbidding stockade of a building, all severe angles, sharp spires, and protruding buttresses. I wondered what sort of architect designed a house like this, let alone who originally wanted to live in it. Small wonder that an incurable mental patient had sprung from the walls of this imitation Bastille in Strawberry Hill Gothic.

As I walked up the sparkling limestone stairs, the door opened and a wispy woman whose face looked the picture of gracefully aging beauty swept down to meet me. I must admit that my first thought on meeting her was that she was hardly the sort of person I could imagine conspiring to keep the sexual molestation of a child a secret, even out of denial. She had a kindness to her, but it was girded with such naturally aristocratic steel that I imagined she'd been born ringing a bell to summon servants.

"Dr. H—," she said in the same prep-school-inflected accent I'd heard over the intercom, "such a pleasure to receive you. Dr. G— called ahead to let me know you'd be coming today, and I must say I was relieved. How is my boy? I have been wondering ever so much about my poor Joseph and haven't heard almost anything from the hospital these past years—other than the bills, of course—so you can imagine my pleasure at your calling. Do please come in."

"Thank you, Mrs. M——," I said graciously, shaking her hand with what I hoped was appropriate professionalism. "I'm very glad to have caught you at home, since I've been hoping to speak to Joe's parents."

"Well, I'm afraid you'll have to make do with me," she said, a touch sadly. "Joseph's father has been dead for the past ten years. However, if I can be of help, I will be happy to do what I can. Just come into the sitting room and we'll talk."

The "sitting room" was actually a high-ceilinged vaulted chamber abundantly furnished in aged mahogany and cherrywood, with what looked to be a few genuine mounted animal heads. Unaccustomed to the trappings of such advanced wealth, I naturally found myself looking around with no small amount of wonder, when one particular mount made me jump back in shock and utter a small gasp.

It was, to be blunt, not the head of anything I had ever seen or wish to see again. If I had found out it was genuine, I might have had nightmares for the rest of my life. Protruding from the plaque to which it was grafted stretched a bulbous, almost shapeless head nearly a foot long bearing a pair of massive, sickly yellow segmented eyes and several rows of pincers that looked like they were dripping with venom. Worse, the taxidermist had evidently set out to make it look as lifelike as possible, because the eyes still flickered with the malignant glare of sadism, and the pincers flared out from the face in an attitude of furious aggression, as if the thing might slam its mandibles shut at any moment and crush the head of whatever innocent creature it had caught in their grip. A yawning, fanged maw like the mouth of the world's largest leech stretched between the pincers and the eyes, ready to eviscerate whatever entered it.

Seeing my horror, Mrs. M—— followed my gaze and shuddered.

"Awful thing, isn't it?" she asked. "I've never had the heart to take it down, though. Don't worry, it's only an artistic piece—nothing real. Charles—Joseph's father, I mean—was quite an accomplished hunter, and when Joseph's night terrors first started, he thought it might help him if we pretended he'd caught and killed the thing and mounted its head in this room. We commissioned an artist to get a description of what it looked like from Joseph himself and to study his drawings. That's what he produced."

She sniffed bitterly. "The hideous thing didn't reassure Joseph, of course. If anything, I suspect it scared him more. But since his long hospitalization, I've kept it here partially to remember how much Charles wanted to see Joseph cured and partially as a sort of symbol of hope for me that one day Joseph might beat the mental illness that made him imagine the filthy thing in the first place."

Still transfixed with disgust and fascination, it took quite a bit of effort to tear my eyes away from that monstrous depiction of a six-year-old's bogeyman. However, the mention of his night terrors did remind me of my purpose, and I turned to look at Joe's mother.

"Mrs. M—, it's actually Joe's night terrors that brought me here," I began, having practiced my pitch several times in the car. "Even though we've tried many courses of treatment with your son, we have begun to wonder if his more lasting psychosis might somehow be connected to his earlier night terrors. We never really explored them when he first came in, and perhaps there's something we would have learned if we'd asked more about them in the first place."

Joe's mother gave me a searching look, and for the first time, it struck me that despite her exceedingly polished appearance, she really appeared quite anxious, even desperate, for some good news.

"Dr. H—, firstly, call me Martha," she said. "If you are serious about trying to bring back my son after all these years, then at the very least, we should be on first-name terms. Ask whatever you like. If I know the answer, I will give it to you."

I nodded. "Thank you, Mrs. M—Martha."

I knew I should ask more about the nightmares, but as I observed the opulence surrounding me, something else came to mind. "First . . . well, I have to wonder. Why did you bring Joe to our hospital?"

Martha laughed lightly. "You think your hospital is too pedestrian for the likes of us? Well, I suppose you've never had to deal with prep school admissions?" I shook my head.

"We were concerned that if we took Joseph to a hospital or doctor who was familiar within our community, the black mark of mental issues would interfere with his eventual application to school and would mar his whole life. My husband and Thomas A— had been classmates at Choate. He agreed to keep Joseph's therapy at CSA a secret as a personal favor. Of course, after a few years, it became clear that the precaution had been pointless. But Charles insisted on keeping Joseph under Thomas's care. We felt reassured by his skill and dedication to our son."

"What were his earliest symptoms? And when did you notice them?"

"Joseph was around five," Martha said. "We had moved to this house and decided it was time for him to have his own room. I was pregnant with his little sister, Eliza, at the time, and while we could have knocked down a few walls and expanded the nursery, all our friends told us that five was too old to be sleeping in a room for babies—it wouldn't be fair for a growing boy to have to put up with a crying newborn. So we had a decorator come in and remodel one of the smaller top-floor suites into the most charming little boy's bedroom you can imagine and put Joseph in there. He absolutely *loved* his new room when he saw it, and his nanny practically had to drag him down to dinner to get him to leave it. But that night . . ."

She swallowed hard and put up a hand. "If you don't mind, Dr. H——, I think I'll pour myself a drink before we continue. Can I get you one as well?"

"Parker, please," I said. "And no, thank you."

She stood up and walked briskly to a hand-carved globe bar and poured an ample amount of amber liquid into a fine crystal glass, which she swirled for a few moments before taking the first sip. Apparently fortified, she sat back down and continued talking.

"That night . . . Parker, you cannot imagine how terrible it was. Joseph began screaming as if he were being murdered barely an hour after we put him to bed. And when we went to check on him, he told us that a giant bug had got hold of his head with its pincers and was going to hurt him. His bedclothes didn't show any signs of damage, and his face was completely unharmed, so we chalked it up to a nightmare from being in a new room. We thought it would go away after that night, but it didn't. It kept happening."

She took another sip of her drink, and this time it was longer and more pained.

"We tried everything," she said emphatically. "At first we thought it was his imagination, but his reaction was so vivid and expressive. We set traps near the wall he said it came from. But they were never sprung when he started screaming, and nothing as big as he described could've avoided it. We asked the nanny to wear him out with physical activities during the day, in the hope he'd sleep more deeply. But then . . ."

She paused, recollecting something that evidently puzzled her.

"Then his *nanny* began acting oddly, so much so that we had to fire her. Yes, I remember now. When we first hired her after we moved in, she seemed like such a sweet and loving caretaker. We needed someone who'd be good with a young boy but also able to handle being a combination night-and-day nurse for an infant when Eliza came along. But then, a few weeks later, we found her shouting profanities at Joe as he cowered in a corner. I suppose his troubles must have worn on her, too, but *whatever* the cause of her ill temper, we couldn't have her taking it out on him. At any rate, we let her go and hired someone who was older. More experienced. We hoped she would be less prone to losing her patience with a little boy's energy. Sadly, she wasn't ideal either after a while. She became sluggish and slow. She was fine with Eliza when she arrived, which I suppose was most important at the time, but she could never keep up with Joseph. So I did my best to tire him out before I got too big with Eliza.

"Every day, we told Joseph we were 'cleaning the monster out' and throwing it away, but he'd insist it was still there. We tried moving him to other bedrooms on his floor, but that didn't help. For one month early on, I brought him into our bedroom, but Charles wouldn't let that stand. For starters, Joseph was still restless and having nightmares, though nothing nearly as potent, and for another, we needed him to learn to sleep on his own. To grow up. At some point, we started sedating him, which seemed to buy him a few hours of rest before he'd wake us all up howling in the early hours of morning.

"Then my husband got in a sculptor to make that *thing* you saw when we first walked in and pretend it had been killed on Joseph's behalf, but that didn't do any good either. We decided that perhaps Joseph was seeing insects around the house and they were triggering the problem, because he was so terrified of insects that just the sight of one would send him into hysterics. So we hired an exterminator to make daily visits and asked him to go over the whole house—especially Joseph's room—every day to kill any bugs that crawled in. Nothing worked. He insisted the monster was waking him by stroking his face with its claws and holding his head in its pincers every night."

Martha nipped her drink. "Charles was insistent that he would get over it eventually, that all little boys have recurring nightmares or see bogeymen of some kind, and that this was no different. He worried that putting Joseph into therapy or bringing him to a mental ward might scar the boy more than whatever he was seeing at night. And he was certain that it would negatively affect his chances at getting into a good middle school.

"But after nine months, it started to get worse. Joseph had grown listless. If a six-year-old could be depressed, I'd say he was. He didn't talk about it as much, and some nights we'd just hear sobbing. But then. Then he came down to breakfast with bruises. It took me a couple of days to realize what it was; I thought it was just rough play with friends. But then there were scrapes, too, all up and down his arms. I realized I could bear it no longer, and I made Charles call Thomas, who had us bring him to CSA."

She finished the last of her drink and, clearly working to maintain her composure, paused and went to the decanter. Turning her back to me, she refilled her glass, and I didn't interrupt. I sensed this was a story that was taking everything she had in her to get out.

"He stayed there. I think a night or two, I don't recall. But when he came home, Parker, you would not believe that little boy had ever been scared of anything. He chattered excitedly the whole way home that he wasn't scared of the monster anymore. That he was brave now, and that the monster was just him scaring himself. 'I'm not scared of me, Mommy, so I can't be scared of it! The doctor in the castle for scared people said so!' That's what he kept repeating."

She smiled wryly, "It seemed as though this was a variation of what Charles had been saying to him for years—that it wasn't real, there are no such things as monsters, he was imagining it—but I suppose it was the effect of Thomas. The effect of a very special kind of doctor. Anyway, we tried to give him the sedatives that night, but he insisted he wouldn't need them. He said he wanted to confront the monster and let it know it couldn't scare him anymore.

I noticed her hands were shaking when she took another sip of her drink. "Well, he did scream at first, but before we got to his bedroom door, he went quiet. We thought maybe this was him facing his fears, that whatever the doctor had told him was working. And when he didn't make another peep that night, we assumed he was finally sleeping peacefully.

"But the next morning, we found Joseph squatting in the corner. He had started making awful noises at us and was . . . was sort of leering at us. The way he looked at me, I didn't know him. It was awful.

"So we took him right back to Thomas," she continued. "And I know this must sound like an awful thing to say, but as soon as he left for the hospital, it was as if a cloud lifted. And I know this is probably nothing but my own desperate need not to feel so helpless, but I . . . I have long worried that I blamed my little boy for what was happening to him. That I didn't love him enough to see him through it. And that's why he is . . . the way he is."

It was inconclusive as far as my theory went, but hearing it described in such grim detail only drove home the tragedy of it. "I don't think you should blame yourself. It's obvious you love him, and I'm guessing your husband did, too," I said. And then I infused a gentle quality into my tone. "If you don't mind my asking, why haven't you visited Joe since he was institutionalized?"

Martha gave me an anguished look. "We wanted to, Parker." She spoke so softly it was almost a whisper. "Believe me, for years, we wanted nothing more in the world. But Thomas wouldn't have it. He told us our presence might upset Joseph, and that Joseph was too erratic for more disturbances. We kept asking when it would be all right, but eventually, Thomas lost patience with us. He practically shouted at us that Joseph—*my little Joey*—was a dangerous lunatic. Unstable. Violent. He told us that he was keeping us safe, as much as Joseph, by keeping us apart. If the situation improved, he said, he'd tell us. But decades went by and it . . . didn't. We eventually gave up hope. I think it broke Charles . . .

"But you are here now." She tried to mask her desperation, but despite her years of stoic WASP breeding, it was obvious.

Listening to her, I felt at once dirty for thinking that what Dr. A— had suspected might be true and desperate to prevent her hope from being in vain. "Martha, I have a favor to ask you. It may help with Joe's treatment."

"Yes," she nodded. "Anything."

"We think Joe might have gotten the idea that, rather than the monster being his imagination, part of him *was* the monster," I said. "That means we need to know as much as we can about its origins and determine any environmental factors. In one of the tapes we have of Joe's therapy sessions, he says that the monster came out of his wall. If you don't mind, I'd like to see his room, and with your permission, I'd like to examine that wall to see if there's anything strange about it. Perhaps for evidence of an infestation that your exterminator might have missed?"

Martha didn't seem to need time to consider. She drained her glass in one gulp, then stood and began to walk out of the room. Seeing that I hadn't moved, she jerked her head impatiently.

"Well, what are you waiting for? The answer is yes. Come along."

It was four long flights up through a stately, yet immaculately appointed home. The lower floors were done mostly in the luxe sage and gold with hardwood floors that I associated with the 1990s, while the narrower, carpeted hallway on the top floor revealed the earthy rust and deep brown of the 1970s. I suspected that any remodeling in the intervening years since Joe's departure was confined to the lower floors. As for Joe's room, it was obvious as soon as I walked in that the room hadn't been lived in, or even entered, in quite some time. Dust caked all the surfaces, and some of the old toys in the room looked like they'd rusted. Even so, it was a room that should've put even a nervous child at ease. Toys were scattered everywhere, ranging from action figures to stuffed animals to extensive model train tracks that ran the length of the room. The walls were painted a deep, relaxing blue, except on one side, where a massive, hyperrealistic mural of a bright red race car had been painted in painstaking detail. The four-poster bed looked less like a bed and more like a cloud given physical form, so layered was it with pillows and a downy comforter. And the floor was covered in lush, soft carpeting of the same soothing blue as the rest of the room.

Nevertheless, Martha hesitated on the threshold, as if the sight of the room alone shook her resolve. Then, a steely look entering her eyes, she walked in and beckoned me toward a ten-foot expanse of wall next to the bed. She pointed at it with a disgusted look on her face.

"This is where Joseph said the thing would come from. Rankly impossible, of course. Even if I believed his monster could exist, it couldn't hide here. This is one of the outermost walls of this part of the house. There's nothing on the other side but open air, not even a small crawlspace."

Her eyes seemed to bounce around the room. She made a small gesture of helplessness and looked at me.

"Thank you, Martha," I said.

She nodded stiffly but graciously. "We have an intercom in the hallway here outside his door. I assume it still works, so call me if you need me." She swept out of the room and closed the door behind her.

And now, there was nothing else to do but investigate the room. I started by going through the seemingly endless supplies of toys, games, and books. There was an obvious absence of anything that bore even faintly insect-like features or touched on subjects related to insects; I found nothing that resembled the horrific thing immortalized in sculpture downstairs. Aside from how numerous they were, there was nothing remarkable about Joe's personal effects. These were just the sort of things you'd expect to see in a wealthy child's room, though the games and books were clearly dated to the early 1970s.

Next, I checked closets and drawers, sifting through boys' clothes. And I checked the bed, but as gingerly as possible, because the dust cloud it would kick up would kill me. As it was, the tang of mold and smell of decay were considerable. It was useful that the place seemed to have been entirely untouched since

Joe's departure, but I hadn't encountered anything significant.

Well, almost. There was one thing that was a bit odd. The vast majority of Joe's toys were broken. This was particularly true of the stuffed animals, which was counterintuitive, seeing as those items are often designed to withstand a child's abuse. And yet, most of the plush toys I found bore obvious signs of having had parts sewn up or back together, or still bore incisions where stuffing was poking out. Theoretically, I suppose these could have been done by a child, but it would have taken some imagination. Particularly so, given that I didn't see any toys or objects that looked obviously sharp or durable enough to do the job. Nor did the sliced-open parts of the stuffed animals correspond to areas where a child would be most likely to stretch or put pressure on them—ears, necks, tails—which raised the question of who or what had opened up these toys to begin with. Was it Joe? Was it his father? An act of sadism meant to harm the child's treasures? Dr. A——'s theory came to mind. But I needed more evidence. I had to look at the wall itself.

At a glance, it didn't seem suspicious. I got between it and the bed and began touching the wall, pressing on it, and knocking on it with a knuckle, looking for signs of softness or deterioration. I studied it for evidence of bugs or other vermin.

My eyes scanned the wall, crossed the floor, and moved up Joe's old bed, then back . . . and noticed there were two areas where the carpet looked slightly uneven. The legs raised the bed about a foot off the floor, so I could just see something underneath.

Wondering if it was a trick of the light, I knelt down and reached out to feel the wrinkling, only to find that the carpet had been partially ripped up from the floor in both places and imperfectly set back in place.

Intrigued, I pulled at what seemed to be the origin point of the rip, and a long stretch of the carpet came loose from the floor, sliding back as easily as if I were pulling up a bedsheet. It was then that I noticed that the floor underneath, rather than being the same handsome mahogany as it was in other parts of the house, was made of some lighter-colored, more modest hardwood that the carpet had been intended to conceal.

I mention this because it was only on account of the wood's light color that I was able to spot a trail of small brown stains that followed the same trajectory as the ripped-up carpet and stopped at the wall behind me. If I'd had any doubt as to what these were, it was immediately destroyed when I discovered a few small shards of hard material near the foot of the bed, which my medical education enabled me to immediately identify as a child's fingernails. A child had been clinging to the carpet so hard that the fingernails had been ripped out when the carpet itself was torn up, leaving a trail of blood that stopped at the wall.

I stood up and stared at the wall for a long moment, then went out to the intercom and summoned Joe's mom. When she came, I showed her the ripped carpet and bloodied floor and asked her if she'd noticed any of this before. Unaware that the carpet had ever been damaged, she was stunned by the sight of blood and had no idea what to make of it. Her eyes followed the trail of blood, then stared at the wall in fright.

I had to wave at her to get her attention. "Martha, I'd like to have a look inside that wall. Would that be OK?"

"Yes . . . um. What do you need?"

"Do you have an axe?"

Ten minutes later, Martha had found a fire axe in an attic box stored under a window in the nursery down the hall. The weapon was beside an old-style wood-and-rope fire escape ladder. After she handed it to me, I encouraged her to wait in the hallway; I didn't know how messy it would be or what I would find.

I grabbed the axe and began my attack, pouring every ounce of strength my muscles could produce into each swing. The plaster and wooden laths resisted, but the sharpness of the blade and the desperation of my assault pushed through both, and a chunk of the interior wall came loose. As it did, it disclosed a gut-freezing horror that made me wonder if I had either already lost my mind or was about to lose it. A terrible stench wafted toward me.

I kept up my attack, bringing down plaster and chunks of wooden lath and studs, until a large, eighteen-inch sheet of gypsum fell forward, revealing a small nook behind it. And inside that space, with the wood sculpted around it so perfectly that it looked as if it had been carved in place, was the tiny skull of a human child.

Horrified, I had to back away from the wall and cover my mouth to keep from retching as the smell of decades of decomposition hidden by that carved-out tomb hit my nose. Worse still was the incredulity I felt. What I was smelling and seeing seemed impossible. There was no way that anyone could have carved a space sized so precisely that it would conceal a child's corpse inside a solid wall so perfectly that you'd have to knock down the wall to find it. There was no point! No purpose! Then, in a sudden cataclysm of horror, it all came together.

I'm not scared of me, mommy, so I can't be scared of it! The doctor in the castle for scared people said so!

I worked out why his delusions kept changing. They shift every time someone calls him a new nasty name.

It goes back in the walls when they come. It melts. Like ice cream. It looks like it is the wall.

I'm going to tell it that it doesn't scare me the next time I see it!

The rush of thoughts that blasted my mind was so terrible I couldn't help screaming aloud. Because in that instant, I knew that what had happened was far worse than anything I, Rose, or Thomas had surmised.

The real Joe had been dead ever since the night after his first return from the hospital. He'd been asphyxiated in a tomb created by hands that could melt through a solid wall, the hands of the Thing that had tormented him. And then, having been told that it *was* Joe, the monster living off his fear and suffering had assumed his form and proceeded to the all-it-could-eat buffet that was our "castle for scared people." There, it had tortured more than two decades' worth of unsuspecting mental patients, staff, and doctors. It had grown fat on years of bad thoughts that it had barely had to work to produce. And with every attempt we made to "cure" that unnamed, malevolent parasite, we had sent it a new victim. If I had held on to any remnant of faith in the ultimate curative powers of science and medicine before then, that revelation destroyed it.

But painful as that was, it also brought a sort of cold clarity. As Martha, Joe's mom, came bursting through the door, I understood I had to find a way to get justice for the poor, murdered boy whose corpse I had just disinterred.

When Martha looked into the hole in the wall, I think her mind must have at first refused to accept what was there. For all she could do was stare—with wide, uncomprehending eyes—at the petite skeleton that had been entombed in that cursed room for so long.

When she finally broke her gaze, it was to look up at me with a childlike expression that seemed to implore me, the doctor, to provide a rational explanation.

"What is the meaning of this?"

I couldn't even begin to formulate an answer, so I didn't try. Instead, I replied with a question of my own. "Mrs. M——, may I keep this fire axe?"

Still looking at me with a mixture of fear and incomprehension, she slowly nodded.

April 27, 2008

Well, folks, this is it. The end of the story that I've kept hidden for over ten years. I'm finally letting out a truth that nearly destroyed my interest in the fields of medicine and psychiatry forever, nearly broke my heart and made me insane, and was the cause of devastation to many people associated with the Connecticut State Asylum. To be honest, this should have been the most difficult part of the story to write, yet because of all the positivity you've shown, I felt nothing but relief in being able to set it down. I realize many of you don't quite interpret my discovery in that wall in Joe's childhood home as I did, but I think you'll understand once you hear this final part.

After my horrifying discovery, the next few hours passed in a haze. I suggested to Martha, half-heartedly, that she call the police, but she seemed to be too much in shock to really hear me. Either way, I felt I should depart her property, especially considering how I'd probably just wiped away whatever traces of hope she'd had that she might get her son back, while also raising all sorts of uncomfortable and sanity-threatening questions about what, exactly, she'd been paying to hospitalize for the past twenty-five-plus years. It was best, I reasoned, if I wasn't the first psychiatrist she talked to after that, so I excused myself and headed for my car.

I recall it being about four in the afternoon when I left that cursed mansion, fire axe in hand, whereupon I immediately drove back toward the hospital. But I didn't head straight there. If there was a way to catch the Thing that called itself "Joe" admitting to what it had done, I wanted to be able to use it, so I stopped off at a Radio Shack near the hospital and bought a mini-recorder and a blank cassette tape that could be stored in my pocket. I figured if it didn't know I had the tape, it might slip up, and I could get it on the record.

Then I drove to the hospital.

I arrived around quarter to six and considered taking the fire axe out of my trunk to end this problem then and there, but my knowledge of the typical staffing procedures stopped me. There would be too many people around to try anything now, and while I did want some sort of revenge on the monster, I also didn't want to be locked up for it.

At that point, my goal wasn't to kill "Joe" but to get some answers out of him. Whatever else he might have been, he was still a prisoner at the mercy of whoever held the key to his room. I stormed into the hospital, and after a detour to my office to grab my lab coat, I headed straight for the cursed creature's lair. Once outside, I snapped the cassette into the machine, pressed Record, and concealed the device in my lab coat pocket. Then I shoved my key into the door and pushed it open furiously, my righteous anger overpowering whatever trace of fear I might have had at facing this unknown agent of terror.

"Joe" looked up as I entered his room. Seeing it was me, his face split into its usual crooked grin, as if nothing whatsoever had happened since my failed attempt to release him. When he spoke, it was in the same rasp he'd used while pretending to be sane.

"Well, well, well, long time no see, doc."

"Cut the crap," I snapped at him. "What are you?"

"*What* am I? Boy, she really did a number on you, didn't she? I told you, I'm a sane man that they're using for mon—"

"Don't you fucking dare," I barked. "I've just gone to the *real* Joe's house. I've seen what was in the wall. I'll ask you again: I know you're not human, so *what are you?*"

This next part I hesitate to write down as I remember it. I have spent years trying to convince myself — with all the tools psychiatry can offer — that what I remember is only my imagination. Nevertheless, the memories stayed stubbornly the same. Therefore, if I am to convey the danger I feel a duty to warn you all about, I have to give my experience the credence it deserves and report it as I recall it, even if I find it more comforting to pretend it was my own mind momentarily abandoning sanity.

"Joe" stared at me for a long moment. My knowledge was a development he evidently hadn't expected. He stood up and raised his hands towards me, exposing his forearms. Wounds opened at his wrists, peeling slowly as if by magic. But it was not blood that flowed from them; it was an avalanche of squirming, writhing, ravenous maggots. His smile widened and kept on widening until his cheeks split apart and opened into a bloody rictus. An ugly, poisonously yellow pool began to form at his feet, with streaks of scarlet floating in its midst. His legs and torso lengthened until he towered over me, staring down with a malignant, nightmarish amusement.

When the Thing that called itself "Joe" opened its mouth again, blood dribbled from its exposed gums, and it laughed with the moist, rotting wheeze from my nightmares. "Parker . . . my baby," it crooned in a distorted, detestable parody of my mother's voice. *"Help me."*

For a moment, I was paralyzed with fear. Had I been a weaker man, had I not seen the small skull and bones in the wall and learned everything of the past day, I might have stayed that way. Might have run gibbering from the room only to be strapped to a gurney myself. But years of survivor's guilt and searing moral outrage had done their work, and I knew in that moment that to fear the Thing was to give it what it wanted. And I could not, *would not*, do that. My fear turned to white-hot rage, and I spat in the mutilated, leering face of the Thing that called itself "Joe."

"Fuck you! You're talking like my mom 'cause you think I'm too scared to fight back. The same way you knew looking like some giant bug would scare the real Joe."

There was no reply, only more blood gushing from the Thing's mutilated mouth. Yet it seemed to want to communicate something. It took everything I had not to back down as it leaned towards me so that I could smell its fetid breath, a movement that didn't seem to precede an attack. It raised one of its long spidery hands and pressed right on the pocket where I had concealed the recorder. Then, with another moist laugh, it wagged its finger at me in mock reproach. The meaning seemed clear: *that won't do you any good.*

Another chill spiked over me. I ignored this one, too, but with more effort. "What are you? I must know."

The Thing's jaw seemed to scrape itself loose, and this time, its dank, decayed voice managed to form words.

"*What . . . do . . .* you *. . . think?*"

It was a trap. It wanted me to give it a new part to play.

"I think you're a fluffy little bunny rabbit," I said in a mocking voice. "I think I'll call you Cuddles."

The Thing gave another horrible, hoarse laugh.

"*You . . . don't . . .*"

It paused for longer than usual as more blood dribbled down its chin.

". . . believe . . . *that.*"

I glared at it.

"Maybe not, but I'm not going to feed you a role. I know how you work," I said. "But I'll tell you what I know. I know you killed Joe. You killed him and took his place."

It didn't reply. For a few seconds, it didn't react at all. Then, with another blood-soaked chuckle, it jerked its head up and down, nodding in agreement. I repressed a shudder.

"Why?" I asked, more out of reflex than real curiosity.

The Thing paused, seeming to seriously consider my question. When its mouth opened to speak again, it was so close I nearly choked on the foul smell of its breath.

"Nothing . . . like . . . me . . . ever . . . got . . . the chance . . . to be . . ."

"To be human?" I finished in a low, horror-struck whisper. It wagged its finger at me again, shaking its head with exaggerated knowingness.

". . . *to be* . . . prey . . ." it finished, laying special emphasis on the last word.

I felt ill, but I forced myself to confront the situation with as much detachment as I could. It was taunting me, but at least it was being honest.

"But why stay here? You could've been free all those years. You could've tortured people without being imprisoned. Why spend so long here?"

"Didn't . . . know . . . how . . . to be . . . prey . . ." the Thing hissed. *"Here . . . so much food. Here . . . safe. Here . . . I learn . . . how prey . . .* think."

It jabbed one finger at its chest, then at me.

"Curious," it wheezed. *"Like . . . you."*

Reflexively, I stepped back, appalled at the implication.

"I'm *nothing* like . . . whatever you are!" I snarled before I could stop myself. Its laughter hacked and wheezed in my ears.

"Yes . . . you . . . are. Both . . . live . . . on . . . misery. You . . . profit. I . . . eat."

"Shut up," I tried to shout, but it came out hollow and tremulous. The Thing was leaning very far into me now, so close it felt grotesquely intimate.

"Could . . . help you. Could . . . show you . . . what . . . other prey . . . fear."

I felt so sick I had to lean against the wall, but I was still defiant. I faced it with all the courage I could muster.

"No," I said. "I know what you're doing. You know my worst fear is not being able to save people. You're just making me think you can help me do that so you can watch me fail and feed on my misery, too."

The Thing's expression—if you could call its mutilated face that—darkened momentarily. However, in a moment, its smile had returned and, with it, a laugh like a waterfall of acid.

"You . . . can't . . . fight . . ." came that hideous croaking burble. *"Stupid prey. You're . . . helpless."*

"More fool you," I said, reckless bravery entering my voice. "It's you that's helpless the way you are now. All you can do is pull parlor tricks to try and scare people, but if that fails, you're up shit creek."

"Then . . . why not . . . try to kill me? Get . . . axe. Come back. Try. I . . . look . . . forward."

Axe? I was momentarily at a loss for words and started to feel intimidation creeping in on my consciousness. Then, a sudden thought crossed my mind, and I returned its mocking, sadistic leer with one of my own.

"I don't need to try to kill you," I said softly. "All I need to do is get everyone here to stop paying attention to you. Which I can do now that I've seen what you did to the real Joe. And really, that's what *would* kill you, isn't it? If we stop sending in orderlies, nurses, and doctors, you'll have no victims. You'll starve to death in here. Well, enjoy whatever bad thoughts you're getting out of me, you fucking parasite, because they're the last ones you're *ever* going to eat. That I promise you." I turned around and was about to leave, when I heard the Thing speak again, this time at a normal speed, and in the normal Joe's voice. And somehow, that only made its last words more dissonant—and disconcerting.

"Doc? Listen to the tape. For your own sake, listen to it before you try anything. Please."

I turned back in spite of myself. "Joe" was looking at me with a fearful expression. All traces of blood and mutilation had vanished from his face and clothes, and he'd returned to his patient's facade. The floor was clean of effluvia, as though a hallucination had passed from me. I didn't give the sight time to scare me. I turned around and slammed the door behind me, leaving the hospital in a rage. When I got back in my car, I pulled out the tape recorder I'd taken in, stopped it, and rewound the tape. Then, as I drove home, I pressed Play to learn what, if anything, I had recorded.

I wish I could say I'd seen the results coming, but unfortunately, even I'd held out some hope that I could gather hard evidence that I wasn't insane.

You've probably guessed what I heard: My own voice and my own angry protestations were preserved clearly on the tape. But the mocking, jeering responses of the Thing that called itself Joe were nowhere to be heard.

Instead, all I could hear was the terrified pleading of a familiar, reedy man's voice, raspy from disuse, but otherwise thoroughly ordinary.

Needless to say, I smashed the tape with a hammer when I got home and threw it away. I was stuck. I couldn't tell anyone what I'd learned. It had effortlessly outmaneuvered me. Without proof that it was an inhuman monster that lived on the fear and suffering of anyone who interacted with it, I could hardly expect the hospital to just give up on feeding and clothing it. As the hours passed, truth be told, I began to doubt everything that had just happened. I wasn't even sure if I was still sane.

I realize that in the movies, this would end with me overcoming my doubts, going back to confront the monster that called itself Joe, and shoving an axe blade through its skull, or something dramatic like that. But unfortunately, while this story certainly had its moments of Hollywood-style horror psychodrama, it doesn't end that way.

I did not go back to the hospital that night. In fact, I'm not sure if I ever went back to Joe's room again, and not for the reason you might think.

Why do I say I'm not sure? Well, that's the last odd part of this story.

When I got home from the hospital after my visit with the Thing that called itself Joe, I found Jocelyn waiting for me. To her credit, she immediately realized that something was wrong and that I wasn't ready to talk about it. So she poured me a few drinks and then held me until I was able to sleep.

And that night, I dreamt I went back to the hospital, but it wasn't lit up the way the hospital should've been at night. Every window was pitch-black, and had I been awake, I would have had no idea how to navigate the place at all. But apparently, the dream knew where I was going, because I felt an implacable force drive me onward. Evidently, my subconscious mind knew the hospital better than I did, because I didn't enter via the main entrance. Instead, I snuck in through a little-known fire exit that somehow had been left open. Ordinarily, I would've been entirely disoriented, stumbling up a flight of stairs in the dark with no idea where they led, but once more, whatever part of my mind was conjuring the vision seemed to know its way, and I didn't miss a step.

My destination, as you've probably guessed, was the room belonging to the Thing that called itself Joe. But the path there didn't feel normal. Perhaps it's because I was barefoot in the dream, but the floor underneath me felt overly slippery. Almost wet, as if the janitor had just been over it with a mop. But this wasn't the most obviously dreamlike feature of the experience. That happened when I got to the room itself, when I heard the latch click and saw the door open by itself.

A horribly familiar echo of a voice cackled from within, and liquid began to gush from the aperture. It poured out of the room, almost as if I'd opened the door to a sealed aquarium, and swept down the hallway in a torrent, accompanied by the sound of hoarse, sepulchral laughter echoing with deafening volume. The liquid smelled of iron, blood, and urine, the awful reek that had haunted my nightmares since I was young. There might have been more to the dream, but the cold, wet sensation rushing against my skin felt so real that it jolted me awake, and I felt Jocelyn frantically shaking me. Apparently I'd woken her up when I started mumbling in a deep, watery voice that scared her so much she had to rouse me. What's more, I must have sweated through my nightclothes, because they felt like dripping rags when I woke up. At least, I tell myself I sweated through them, because the alternative is just too unnerving.

When I went to the hospital the next day to see Dr. G— and share with her what I'd learned at Joe's house, I discovered an electrician's van as well as several police cruisers in the parking lot. I thought something serious must be happening and noticed that the staff and patients appeared to be rattled as I hurried to the medical director's office on the upper floor.

I found the doctor meeting with a few staff members, but she shooed them out and brought me in so we could speak alone.

"I want to know what happened on your trip yesterday," she said, strain evident in her voice. "But first you need to know . . . Last night a pipe appears to have burst on the second-floor ward, and the water flooded a nearby breaker. The breaker is centrally and internally located because it's a rather vital link in the system and isn't supposed to be vulnerable to little things like bad weather or disasters. The electrician was able to come by and fix it, but the whole hospital was blacked out for somewhere between ninety minutes and two hours. And during that blackout, someone broke into the hospital and unlocked the door of a patient's room—Joe's room—as well as the doors to his secure ward."

"Unlocked it? Someone let him out?" My voice was shrill. "Did you catch them? Did you catch *him?*"

Her expression altered a touch, as if something in that moment was settled for her. "Yes, someone did. No, we did not catch them. Unfortunately, the blackout affected the security cameras. And no, we did not apprehend him. Joe has escaped."

April 30, 2008

I realize that was a shorter post. After I typed those last words, "Joe has escaped," I set aside my computer and had to go dark for a while. Some things happened that day that still haunt me and are particularly difficult to share. I wasn't sure I would, especially in light of the reaction I received—I see many of you are vociferous in your negative views of my last post—but I think I need to be as honest as I know how to be with you, regardless of what you choose to believe. Now, you've heard the meat of the mystery, but the conclusion is revelatory as well.

The police questioned me as a suspect in his escape, of course. Security footage showed I'd visited Joe's room for twenty minutes earlier that evening, at around six, and Hank, the orderly assigned by

Dr. G— to keep me under surveillance, had reported that I'd been in Joe's room and he'd heard me arguing with him. Hank had looked in the door's window, but whatever he saw inside reassured him that we weren't in danger of hurting each other, which I took to mean he saw nothing of Joe's transformation. In addition, there was a witness statement from Dr. P— that I'd *possibly* tried to help Joe escape the day prior. But Jocelyn confirmed my alibi that we went to bed together the night before, and, as I learned much later, Dr. G— made a statement on my behalf explaining that my actions during the previous "escape" attempt had been a study of the patient with her knowledge. Therefore, I was soon ruled out as a suspect. The hospital staff, particularly the orderlies Marvin and Hank, were slower to believe in my innocence, but I was too preoccupied to care when they looked askance at me.

The irony of the situation is that the police believed someone set out to harm Joe. It is hospital policy to notify the authorities if a patient, even one who's voluntarily committed, escapes. The concern is that Joe was released because someone wished to prank him, or worse. Joe has no criminal record with the police; according to them, he is nonviolent. And most of the hospital community may have loathed Joe or stayed away from him, but they hadn't been there long enough to know of the assaults he'd committed as a child. The patients and staff in the institution who had heard rumors about Joe—that people went crazy around him—didn't speak up for fear they'd be mocked. The police are on the lookout for an adult male they believe is unwell and needs care.

They have no idea.

My discussion that day with Dr. G— was interrupted by the news that something was wrong with her mentor, Dr. A—. She had to leave abruptly, so I didn't have a chance to report what I'd learned at Joe M—'s home, the skeleton I'd found in the walls of the child's bedroom. Nor did I tell her about my evening confrontation with the abomination that had confirmed my findings but left me with no usable recorded evidence. At any rate, Dr. G— was inconsolable and disengaged from the hospital in the coming weeks, so I never found an opportunity to speak with her again. Apparently, Dr. A— had succumbed to heart failure at his home. He was found by a housekeeper the next morning, sprawled on the floor of his kitchen, and the authorities believe his symptoms were violent and terribly painful. A chair had been knocked over, and near the body was a smashed mug or teacup in a scattering of the papers he must have been reviewing.

About a week later, I received a message from the medical director via Dr. P—, who, of all people, had grown strangely upbeat and energetic with the departure of the patient he knew as Joe. It was as though my colleague and I had traded places. I felt discombobulated and depleted, uncertain our work was worthwhile in the face of the damage I saw all around us, while Dr. P— was animated by renewed vigor. Still, he wasn't verbally abusing me, so I accepted the change with equanimity. The message he brought from Dr. G— was a report that Martha M—, Joe's mother, had committed suicide. A gardener found her two, or possibly three, days after Dr. A— died. It seems she leapt from the window in her son's bedroom. There was no mention of anything untoward found in the house or in the bedroom. No mention of a hole chopped in the wall or a crypt for the bones of her young son. I've no idea what to make of that, and since I hadn't seen Dr. G— since, I was unable to ask her.

The hospital regained some measure of normalcy within the next two weeks or so, but I was in an anxious funk. Despite my record as the one doctor who had come away unscathed after working with Joe, I was an abysmal failure. And there was one more calamity to come.

About two weeks after the fiend disappeared, I was woken by campus police and brought to the university hospital, where I found a bruised and bloodied Jocelyn. The instant I looked at her, I knew everything was wrong. Her normally bright and expressive green eyes were dead and glassy. Her hair was disheveled and tangled. Her expression was manic and brittle, in a way that shocked me. When I tried to put my arms around her to comfort her, she recoiled, as if the very thought of being touched made her ill. Then, slowly, she melted into my arms with a crooked, broken smile that spoke all too clearly that she'd experienced something profoundly traumatic.

The police explained that Jocelyn had been attacked after leaving the library that evening. When asked about her assailant, as you may have already guessed, she described a slight man with scraggly blond hair and unfocused eyes—in other words, to my mind, the human form taken by the Thing that called itself Joe. I could only assume it had somehow followed me into the city.

When I heard that, it took every ounce of sanity I had for my mind not to crumble. How could I, a man who had begun medicine because I couldn't bear the sight of one of the most significant women in my life, my mother, being broken by neglect, have let the other one be similarly broken by *my* neglect? It was agonizing to think about, and all the more so because of how deeply I loved Jocelyn, and how much it ached to see her wounded in such a primal, irreversible way. Had she not been severely injured and in need of hospital care, I might have run away from New Haven, from her, and from my entire adult life right then, knowing that the one thing I felt that I was put on this earth to do—to heal and protect people—had been the cause of my failing someone I loved. I realize how unreasonable that probably sounds, but in all fairness, I was an emotional mess.

It was impossible to deny the peril that I may have inadvertently brought to Jocelyn—and the whole world—even for a moment, and almost as terrible was the complete *senselessness* of it all. Just when I thought I had the fiend figured out, it surprised me again. I had thought it wanted to be locked up, surrounded by the psychologically miserable in our hospital, so why escape now? It had been living comfortably on that ward for decades and had easily neutralized the threat I posed. Why risk its luck outside?

Unfortunately, I did eventually come up with a theory for this last question, and it instantly filled me with guilt. As I recalled the last conversation between me and the Thing, I remembered that its reason for staying in the hospital was that it "didn't know how to be prey," which is to say, how to act human. What's more, it didn't change its shape in response to my "fluffy bunny rabbit" taunt because I "didn't believe it." Furthermore, even though all its means of inflicting psychological torture relied on knowledge a human couldn't have, they were still methods that a human could use. Therefore, the only conclusion I could draw was that as long as everyone on staff treated the Thing as if it were human, it had to go along with their perception.

So in his own terribly sad way, poor little Joe had imprisoned it by making it pretend to be human. True, one patient had called it a "fucking monster," but it must have sensed that he meant a metaphorical monster, not a literal one. The patient didn't believe it was inhuman, so it couldn't change. And as long as no one else called its bluff, it was trapped in that form.

But then I had to come along and tell it that not only did I believe it wasn't human; I *knew* it wasn't. Which meant that I must have freed it to assume the most effective shape, whether it was a monster, a person, or the wave of piss and blood I had felt in my dream. And with its ability to shapeshift restored, it had no need to rely on our hospital as a sanctuary where people were trained not to believe in monsters.

Such was, and is, my theory for why it escaped. Sadly, there is likely no way I'll ever prove or disprove it, which means that it will weigh on my conscience, unresolved, forever.

May 1, 2008

I thought the April 30 post was truly my final one, but I simply cannot leave things on such a negative note. I want you to know where we stand now, and what I've done to try to make amends in this world.

Jocelyn was deeply scarred by her assault. She spent a couple of days in the hospital, then retreated to our bedroom for further recovery, only to fall into a cataclysmic depression. When she began insisting she had no desire to finish her doctorate, even going so far as to smash her computer and backup discs in front of me, I introduced the idea of moving. We needed our own escape.

Jocelyn dropped out of her program, and I decided to go into private practice. My contacts from residency and medical school enabled us to move. I'll admit it's out of the region, but I don't wish to say where. Assault and trauma change a person. For a long time, I barely recognized Jocelyn, and I suspect she felt the same about me. Still, our love was enduring, so we married about eighteen months later. Every day, we learned each other anew. Our scars are still with us, and I can see Jocelyn still fighting depression. She presents a happy aspect to me but has become a devoted homebody and displays no interest in making new friends. She says I am all she needs.

For my part, I have always needed to make a more meaningful contribution. Maybe because I didn't grow up cushioned by wealth as Jocelyn did, or maybe because I know I bear responsibility for my part of this story, I will spend the rest of my years atoning.

To that end, I've been using the knowledge I gained from that one patient in the best way I can. I've opened a boutique psychiatric practice that specializes in treating children with paranoid delusions or fear disorders. Some have been fairly standard cases, while others have involved shared delusions, like the boy whose parents thought he was being haunted by his stillborn sister's ghost.

Every now and then, I get a child who tells me about a monster that won't let them sleep. Sometimes it comes from the wall. Sometimes it comes from the closet. Sometimes it comes from under the bed. But wherever it comes from, it's always the thing they're most afraid of. Except now there's another detail, which makes sleep difficult, even for me: sometimes, the monsters goad their victims, saying they're just children who've been turned into monsters and asking the children they torment to "free" them by telling them they're people, too. Worse, sometimes I'm not sure if those children are really even asking for my help, or if they even are children. Perhaps they are fiends similar to Joe, gloatingly showing off their handiwork to the one person who would know what they are and how to stop them. Sometimes I think they're laughing in my face behind those terrified, ostensibly innocent children's eyes.

But whatever the reason these youngsters tell me their stories about what terrorizes them at night, the fact is that some of them definitely are human children. And those defenseless, desperate babes and their families are the people for whom I'm in medicine. Because unlike other doctors, I know what the stakes are. Maybe I'm paranoid, too, but I remember the monster's words. I remember how it exulted that *nothing like me ever got the chance to be prey*, and I shudder at the connotations of those first three words, because I know what they mean: whatever "Joe" was, he wasn't the only one. There might be an entire species of those things living alongside us and only now waking up to the fact that they can live *among* us.

Well, I'll be damned if I let another one take over a child's life. And I guess my suspicions are usually right, because the kids I treat who do suffer from those sorts of nocturnal visitations rarely need a second session after I'm done with them.

Until now, only Jocelyn knew this story. And she believes me. She has been emphatic in her desire that I tell it to someone, so insistent that sometimes I think she seems hungry for it. Until recently, I've always told her no.

But just a few months ago, before I started writing this, she told me she was pregnant. And this time, when she asked me to write this story for an audience, she had a damn good reason.

"I want you to remember what a good man you are, Parker," she said to me. "You don't understand that you're the best thing that ever happened to me. You don't get how free I feel with you. How much I like the person I am with you, despite everything that's happened. And maybe you never will. But if you don't know you're a good man, how can you trust yourself to be a good father to our children? Who knows? Maybe if you tell this story, you'll be able to forgive yourself. And besides, would a good man let the world go on being ignorant about the things you know?"

Hearing Jocelyn say that, for just a moment, I glimpsed the woman I'd fallen in love with hiding behind the manic, crooked smile she's worn since her ordeal. With that flash of recognition, I knew I couldn't refuse her.

So here I am, typing this out and praying you'll believe me. If you don't, that's fine. I'm not sure I believe it myself, or if this is just an episode of some larger psychosis that one day will drive me as insane as my patients. But if you're parents, or psychiatrists yourselves, and you have patients or children who are telling you stories like the real Joe's, then this is the warning I am obligated by medicine and by my common humanity to give you:

Whatever you do, don't tell your child that the monsters they see are only things they created with their imaginations. Because if even a little bit of this story is true, you might be signing their death warrants.

Thanks for reading.

All my best,

Parker

Acknowledgments

Firstly, thank you to Jaime Levine at Houghton Mifflin Harcourt (HMH) Books and Media, who gave me the gift of an editor I could trust implicitly with my mind's output, knowing she would sharpen and darken it to perfection. Thank you as well to Dr. Harrison Levine for answering innumerable questions about psychiatric practice from an enthusiastic amateur. All mistakes are either mine or what Joe demanded for the telling of his story. I also wish to thank Katie Kimmerer, HMH managing editor, as well as Laura Brady, manuscript and copy editor. Additionally, my gratitude to Wendy Muto at Westchester Publishing Services for guiding *The Patient* through the nuts and bolts of the production process.

Also at HMH, thank you to my publicist, Michelle Triant, who has fielded all my panicked emails with expert aplomb. Thank you to my marketer, Hannah Harlow; HMH publisher Bruce Nichols; HMH editorial director Helen Atsma; editorial assistant Fariza Hawke; and Tommy Harron and the audio team; as well as Ed Spade, Colleen Murphy, and the entire sales department. Additional thanks to Ellen Archer, HMH trade president; Lori Glazer, senior vice president of publicity; Matt Schweitzer, senior vice president of marketing; Becky Saikia-Wilson, associate publisher; Jill Lazer, vice president of production; Kimberly Kiefer, production manager; Emily Snyder, design supervisor; and Christopher Moisan, art department director. On that note, last but not least, thank you to Mark Robinson for the superbly claustrophobic and disturbing cover design for this title.

Thank you to my manager, Josh Dove, at Stride Management, for taking a chance on me before I thought I deserved one; to my film/television agent, Holly Jeter, at William Morris Endeavor (WME), who managed my entrance into the bright, scalding lights of Hollywood; and to my literary agent, Joel Gotler, at Intellectual Property Group, who stands as the guardian of my creativity in the literary world. Also at WME, thank you to June Horton and Beau Levinson for negotiating tirelessly on my behalf and for braving the slings and arrows of Hollywood's legal system. Thank you to Ryan Reynolds and Roy Lee, who changed my life forever when they decided to bring my little monster-that-could to the big screen.

Thank you to the many friends who inspired characters and encouraged me to put them on paper. In particular, thank you to my Dungeons & Dragons group (you know who you are), who first pushed me to try my hand at writing fiction. Thank you to McKenna, without whom the patient would not have gotten his name. Thank you to my mother for keeping my imagination alive through childhood and for never ceasing to believe in it even when I had. Thank you to Stephen, the father I should have had. Thank you to Sophie, who relentlessly forced me to keep honing and believing in my skill as a writer. Thank you to IHOP for the bottomless iced coffees that kept me writing the first four chapters of this story before I ever thought of sharing it with the world.

Finally, thank you to every Reddit user who upvoted this story when it made its debut in December of 2015. Without you, *The Patient* would never have been finished. Without you, it would not be where it is today. Without you, I would be a different man. From the bottom of my heart, thank you.